MW00878079

EMINENT DOMAIN

Tit Elingtin

Erin O'Riordan

© April 2011 Erin O'Riordan and Tit Elingtin

All rights reserved

All rights reserved. No part of this book may be reproduced or transmitted in any form or by any means, electronic or mechanical, including photocopying, recording, or by any information storage and retrieval system, without permission in writing from the publisher.

This is a work of fiction. Names, characters, places and incidents are solely the product of the author's imagination and/or are used fictitiously, though reference may be made to actual historical events or existing locations. Any resemblance to actual persons, living or dead, business establishments, events or locales is entirely coincidental.

Special thanks to:

Dara Bettencourt, Editing

Karen Saverine, Formatting

This book is dedicated to all the patriots who fought for our freedom and liberty. The line between patriot and terrorist is drawn by the historian.

One – Death's Eve
December, 2011

Jeff woke up at six a. m. He hated using alarm clocks and always got up without one. He lay there looking at Kendra, marveling at how much he loved her. He knew this was going to be his last day with her and wondered if he could really go through with it.

He went to the bathroom, took a piss, and headed out to the office to log onto Facebook and watch the morning news. He looked out the window at the dark sky and watched the lights reflecting off the black river. The city lights sparkled like a sea of diamonds in the ripples of the water's current. He flipped on the TV and turned on his computer.

He checked his e-mails, but didn't find anything interesting. The weather man said it would be unusually warm the next few days. He wondered if everyone would have a white Christmas.

For the next hour, he played poker on the computer and continued to watch television. After the first twenty minutes of the Today show, he took his morning shit. Then he went into the bedroom and climbed across the bed on top of Kendra, hugging and kissing her.

"Time to wake up, baby doll," Jeff said.

"Ooh," she groaned. "Hi, baby pie." Kendra kissed Jeff back and smiled.

"Hi," Jeff said. "We have a busy day. It's nice out, so do you want to go for a walk?"

Kendra giggled. "Go for a walk, go for a walk!" She panted like a dog. They both laughed as she got out of bed. They got dressed and soon made it out the door. They walked a mile and a half, from Cedar Street to Logan Street. Most mornings they walked to Logan and back. It took an hour. During the walk, they talked about the plans they had for the day, as they did almost every day. Kendra had to be at the airport for an eleven a. m. flight to Chicago. From there she would catch a Metro train to Joliet, Illinois.

"I can hardly believe you're not going with me. I haven't slept without you for almost eleven years," Kendra said.

"I know it'll be weird. I'm sorry; I can't sit on the plane and train all that time. My kidneys are killing me," Jeff said.

"Yes, literally," Kendra said. "You know you can have one of mine. I'm happy to share."

"I know, baby," Jeff said. "We'll have to talk to the doctor about that."

"You mean you'll have to talk to him. This will be the first time I haven't been there with you," she said.

"Yes, I'll have to ask him." Jeff knew he wasn't going to show up for his appointment. He had other plans. He had made a habit of always being honest with Kendra. He knew he was lying to her, making her believe he was going to his appointment. He couldn't tell her the truth. Not this time. He knew she would stay home to stop him. He knew she loved him like no one else ever had. Tears began to fall down his cheeks. "It'll be okay," Jeff said. "It will all be okay."

Kendra looked at Jeff and saw the tears as he wiped them away. "What's wrong?"

"Oh, nothing," Jeff said, "I was thinking about how I'm going to miss you."

"Well, I'll be back Saturday afternoon. It'll be Christmas Eve. Oh, I'm going to miss you too," Kendra said.

Near the end of their walk, Jeff and Kendra went to Carol's, a downtown diner, for breakfast. Jeff got his usual, a bowl of grits stacked with pepper jack cheese, crispy bacon, two eggs medium and butter. They called it the "special grit bowl" in the kitchen. Jeff was the only one who got his grits like that. Kendra got French toast.

When they finished breakfast they walked home and made love. "I'm going to be late," Kendra said, as they got into the shower. "It's almost ten o'clock."

"Don't worry," Jeff said, "I'll get you there in time."

They finished showering and quickly got dressed. Kendra had packed the night before; Jeff grabbed her bag and threw it in the back of the car. "Are you sure you have everything?" he asked.

"Yes, I'm sure. Do you think we'll make it in time?"

Jeff laughed. "I've been driving you around for eleven years and you have to ask?"

Jeff had a knack for driving like he was playing a video game. He knew the positions of all the cars ahead of, behind and to both sides of him, anticipating the moves of the other drivers. They made it to the Willow Bend Regional Airport in record time. Jeff parked the car and told Kendra, "You get to the check-in counter. I'll be right behind you." Kendra complied. He grabbed her bag.

After getting her bags checked and getting to security, Jeff grabbed Kendra's arm and spun her toward him, catching her by the waist. He gave her a tight hug and said to her in a soft voice, "I love you so much. Without you I'm nothing."

"I love you too, honey pie," Kendra said. "You stay out of trouble while I'm gone."

"We'll see," Jeff said with a wink. "Call me when you get there."

"Okay!" Kendra said as she turned and went through security to the plane waiting on the tarmac.

Jeff watched her go, climbing the stairs of the plane, knowing it was the last time he would see her. He left the building and returned to his car. When he got in it he broke down crying for what seemed like forever. He gained his composure and drove home.

Jeff had the day planned. He still had his fishing boat in the river. He got his pole, fishing tackle and a few beers and headed out the door. He motored the boat over to the waterfall a hundred yards from the house. Gently Jeff bumped the back of the boat against the buoy cable stretching across the river above the waterfall. He set the engine to idle, just fast enough to stay ahead of the current. Looking to his left he saw Charlie and Monk. "Hey, fellas. How's it going?" Jeff said over the roar of the waterfall.

Monk let out a raspy, "Eh, same old, same old."

Charlie gave a wave and said, "You gonna get that big one today?"

"If you don't get it first," Jeff said. "Are they biting?"

"Nah," Monk grunted.

Jeff rigged his line and cast it in. He placed his pole in its holder and sat in his chair. Reaching into his cooler, he grabbed a beer and cracked it open. This is heaven, Jeff thought. If it could be this for the rest of his life, he would have been happy. He thought of all of the fighting he had to do with city government. He got lost in his mind, imagining his house was going to be gone. He would have no more walks in the park, steps from his door. His access to the water would be gone. His future dreams of having a boat rental business were gone.

Jeff swiveled in his seat and looked back at his house. He imagined it gone. All his labor, his effort, felt like a waste of energy now.

Just then Charlie yelled, "Fish on!" as he pointed at Jeff's pole.

"Oh shit!" Jeff said, spinning around in his chair. He dropped his beer and grabbed his pole. The reel drag wailed with clicks as it spun. Jeff tightened the drag a little and started pumping his pole, fighting the fish. "God damn! It's a big one!"

Monk and Charlie grabbed their rods and reeled them in to keep from getting snagged up in Jeff's line. They watched Jeff fight, cheering him on. They kept saying, "Use that drag! Take your time! Don't break the line!" Jeff felt like he was at a ball game. He was loving every moment.

Twice the fish flew out of the water, letting them see its size. "Holy shit!" Monk said.

"Did you see that?" Charlie screamed. "Did you see that? I've never seen one that big. Oh my god, that's a record king salmon!"

After twenty minutes, Jeff got the behemoth up to the boat. He grabbed his net and scooped up the fish. Lying on the deck, it flopped around in the net. Jeff reached over and grabbed a tire buddy he kept on the boat and clubbed the fish in the head, killing it. He reached into the net, grabbed the fish by the gills and held it up for Monk and Charlie to see. "How's that?" Jeff said.

"Wow, it's got to be over twenty pounds. Are you going to weigh it?" Charlie asked.

Monk shook his head, speechless, grabbed his rod and cast his line in. Jeff grabbed his knife, cut the head off the fish and threw it into the water. Then he squeezed it near its rear, pouring out a hand full of roe. He put his hand to his mouth and ate. He took his knife and gutted the fish, throwing the guts in the river. He skinned one side of it and cut a steak-size piece of meat off of it. He rinsed his hands, grabbed another beer and ate his fish steak raw as he sat and watched Monk and Charlie fish.

"Well, good luck, fellas." Jeff said as he got ready to leave. "There's got to be a few more of 'em out there for ya."

"God damn," Monk said in his raspy voice. "I never seen anything like that before."

"You take care of yourself, Jeff," Charlie added.

Jeff motored back up to the house and docked his boat. He finished off the last beer and grabbed the fish.

Returning to the house, Jeff wrapped the rest of the fish and put it in the fridge. Then he got a couple of contractor-sized garbage bags. He went to his closet and put all of his clothes, shoes and toiletries in the bags. He loaded them into the car and took them to the Goodwill store.

Jeff stopped at a Hallmark store and browsed the cards. He wondered what would be best to get Kendra. Should he get a sympathy card, thank-you card, an I-love-you card...he even considered a get-well-soon card. He settled with an apology card. On the cover was a boy in tears with the caption, "I'm so sorry I hurt you." He opened the card; inside it said, "I hope you can forgive me."

That will be perfect, Jeff thought.

Jeff went home. He got a beer and a shot of Jack Daniels, sat at the dining room table and thought of what to write. He downed the shot, chased it with some beer and grabbed a pen. He began writing:

"Thank you for loving me. I never knew true love until I met you. It's breaking my heart to leave you. I'm sure your heart is broken now too. I was so tired of fighting. I hurt physically all of the time and I'm internally in a rage about the city almost always. I know I could have done things differently; I'm just done. Of all people I think you will understand.

"You are a strong woman now, not the insecure, introverted, spoiled brat I married. You know adversity and know how to fight for success. You will do great in this world as you carry on. Be careful. Remember: they all want to fuck you. Few will love you. I do and did.

Love, Jeff"

Jeff read the card a few times and then put it in its envelope. Time for his last meal. He thought of what to have: Pittsburgh style-steak and lobster at Cloverfield's East. It was Wednesday; he knew Lex wouldn't be there. Since Lex never properly apologized, Jeff and Kendra had always avoided going in there when Lex was working. He thought if that little asshole couldn't show him proper respect he didn't want anything to do with him. Lex had made everyone believe that Jeff was going to hurt Lex. Since Lex came across as the nicest guy ever, people hated Jeff for that. He was defamed at his favorite watering hole.

Jeff walked downtown and went in the back door of the restaurant. He walked past the kitchen and saw his favorite cook. "Hey Jim!" Jeff said. "How's it goin'?"

Jim turned his head and saw Jeff. "Hey, how you doin'?"

"Doin' good, doin' good," Jeff said "Glad to see you at the grill. You do the best Pittsburgh steak ever. Burn the hell out of it tonight. Black and medium rare."

A flame shot up from the grill. "You got it, Jeff!" Jim said.

Jeff walked into the dining room, saw Amy, the hostess, and asked her, "Can I sit at that booth there?"

"I don't know. Can you?" Amy asked, laughing.

Jeff smiled big and said, "Okay, smartass, may I?"

"Yes, you may," Amy said.

Jenny said from across the room, "Hey Jeff, can I get you a beer?"

"I hope so!" Jeff replied, "Guinness, please."

"Where's your lady?" Amy asked.

Jeff sat down at the booth. Only a few other tables had customers at them and things were very casual. "She's at a business conference. I'm on my own tonight."

Jeff soon got his beer and ordered his salad and meal. When his steak, lobster and fries arrived he got a bottle of A-1 steak sauce and drowned the fries in it. He took his time, enjoying talking with Jenny as she came by to check on him. He had always had a slight crush on her. He'd told Kendra many times how much he liked Jenny. He'd tease Kendra about fantasies with the two of them. Kendra never seemed to mind. She had once asked Jeff if he ever wanted any other women and he replied, "I want to fuck 'em all." Kendra's response was, "As long as I'm there."

After Jeff finished his meal he moved up to the bar. He sat on the bar stool he called his "Norm seat." Steve was bartending. He said, "Hey buddy, how's it going?"

"Good, Steve. How have you been?" Jeff asked.

"What can I get you?" Steve said.

"Guinness, please, and a shot of Gentleman Jack."

Jeff loved talking with Steve. He sat there drinking for an hour. Kendra called while he was at the bar and they talked for a while too. Jeff told her about his fishing adventure and said he would call her when he got home. It was a little after eight o'clock, and Jeff decided to call it a night. "You can total me out," Jeff said to Steve, giving him his credit card. Jeff wrote $300 in the tip slot and gave Steve instructions: "You keep a hundred. Give Jim and Jenny a hundred each, okay?"

"Wow! You bet, Jeff," Steve said.

Jeff said his goodbyes to everyone and went to the back door. It was raining. He paused there, thinking about calling a cab for the four-block journey. Jenny came around the corner.

"Thanks, hun, for the tip. That was awesome. You have no idea how much I needed it."

Jeff said, "No problem. You deserve it. Are you going out for a smoke?"

"No, going home. I'm done for the night. What are you doing?" Jenny asked.

"It's raining. I'm thinking about calling a cab. It's too cold to walk home wet."

"I'll give you a ride. Come on."

Jeff didn't hesitate. He followed Jenny out to her car, parked nearby. She pushed the unlock button on her key fob and they jumped in out of the rain.

Jeff said, "I live on Cedar Street. The bridge is in my front yard."

"I know where you live. I've been there before," Jenny said.

Jeff looked surprised. Jenny said, "When Lex lived there I was there a few times. Please don't say anything, but I think it's awful how he's treated you and Kendra."

Jeff said, "I won't say anything. Thank you. He'll learn someday. I can't be invested in him anymore. He treats me like I'm second class and I won't put up with that."

Jenny said, "I don't blame you. I have to stay out of it since he's my boss." Jenny pulled into Jeff's driveway and turned off her car. "I'd love to see what it looks like now that you've finished it," she said.

Jeff stopped, his hand on the door handle. "I'd love to let you, but Kendra's not here. I've always had a thing for you, Jenny, but Kendra and I have an agreement: no one of the opposite sex in the house without the other one being here. I love her too much to break my rule. I'm sorry. I hope you understand."

"Kendra's a lucky woman to have you," Jenny said.

"You tell her that next time you see her. She knows I like you. She'll be fine with knowing you said that. She'll know you brought me home. I tell her everything." Jeff winced, knowing he was keeping a big secret from Kendra. He exited the door and said, "You have a good night, Jenny. Thanks for the ride."

"Thank you for the tip!" Jenny said.

Jeff went into the house. Grabbing his cell phone from his pocket he called Kendra. "Hi, baby. I miss you." He told her everything that had happened since they last talked. They talked for an hour. Jeff sat in what he called "The Helm," a bay window area on the second floor that looked out to the river. He sat in his favorite chair, drinking Jack Daniels, and passed out.

Two - Opening the Door
8:27 a. m. the next day

Jeff had cased the home and neighborhood weeks earlier; the city planner, Erin Clarke, owned one of the biggest homes in this part of the subdivision. The house had been built in the '90s; the original, blue-gray roof and matching siding remained.   The two-story home had an attached, two-car garage. If Jeff had to guess, he'd say it had four bedrooms, at least.

He pulled his car into the driveway and parked near the garage. He hadn't seen any of Erin's neighbors along the cul-de-sac as he pulled up. This part of the subdivision lay on a golf course; she had one neighbor on each side, but behind the house, a narrow strip of trees separated the houses from the fairway. Not that it mattered much if the neighbors saw Jeff; they would think Erin hired him to do some work.

He took a battery-powered reciprocating saw from the back of the car, then went around to the back of the house. He climbed under the deck and looked inside a window, making sure he had a good, clear place to get into the walk-out basement without setting off a motion detector. He had an idea of where the plywood sheeting stopped and the insulating foam board sheeting began.   He cut through the siding, the insulation, and straight through the drywall. He removed a one foot by two foot area of the wall. He laughed, thinking to himself how foolishly they'd built this place as he cut through it like a hot knife through butter.

The hole didn't need to be very large, only large enough for Jeff to climb inside without needing to touch a window or a door. That way, he wouldn't set off any of the sensors. The saw made a lot of noise. None of the neighbors poked their heads out of the door to ask him what he was doing. He knew from years of construction work that people rarely asked questions. No wonder homes get burglarized, he thought. People don't care to get involved.

Jeff pulled the remaining foam board and drywall toward the exterior. He set down the reciprocating saw inside the hole, dropping it a foot or so onto the flooring. Then he stepped through the hole. He fit tighter than he'd imagined, and he caught the sleeve of his coat on a nail sticking out of a stud. The sleeve tore, but Jeff made it into the house.

Jeff knew the alarm technicians would have installed the alarm box in the basement near the electric panel. He'd made a mental note of the electric panel's location on his way in. Next to the panel sat the alarm box. Like many homeowners, the Clarkes left their key in the box. He unlocked the box. He followed the wires from the box to the electric outlet it was plugged into. He knew he could unplug the box and the alarm system would act no differently than if the power went out. He also knew the battery inside the box had to be disconnected for the alarm not to send a signal. After unplugging the box, he reached in, grabbed the battery and pulled the terminals at the same time, disconnecting the power.

Jeff located the gas line next. He hesitated for a moment. Was he really going to do this? He'd already broken into the city planner's home. Even as a child, with little supervision and his run of the city, he'd never gotten into anything this illegal before. He asked himself if he was willing to take this final step. Once he crossed this line, he was no longer a good citizen, full of righteous indignation at the actions of his government. This would make him a criminal. He'd been fantasizing about revenge against the government for years now, but this was reality.

He was really about to disconnect the flexible gas line leading into the city planner's house and let the house fill up with natural gas. By the time Erin Clarke got home from working that night, nothing would be left of her home but a burnt-out pile of rubble.

"She deserves it," Jeff said, taking the gas line in his hand. "She deserves to know what it feels like to lose something precious. She deserves to know what it feels like to lose your home and everything you've worked so hard to keep." He decided to see himself as a patriot. This was righteous, he told himself, when the whole system was so corrupt. "Today will be a good day to die."

He cut the gas line with his reciprocating saw and bent the pipe out of the way so the gas could flow freely. He knew something later in the day would trigger the spark that would cause an explosion. He left the utility room, went up the stairs and opened the door to the main floor of the house.

Leaving his saw behind, Jeff hurried up the stairs. With nothing left to stop him, he walked boldly through Erin's house. He turned the thermostat down to fifty-five degrees, assuming once it got cold enough, the call for heat would ignite the house. He looked back on his work with pride as he stopped to take a piss on a potted plant in the foyer. He could already smell the gas and imagined it would only be an hour or two before the house exploded.

He walked out the front door and to his car.

Adrenaline raced through Jeff's veins, but he knew he couldn't drive like a maniac on his way to town hall. He had to make it without getting stopped by the police. As he drove, Jeff dialed the phone number he'd stored in his phone years before, the number he'd used many times to complain about town matters.

A woman's voice came on the phone. "Mayor's office."

"Hi, this is Jeff Gray. Is the mayor in?"

"What is this concerning?" the woman asked.

Jeff replied, "My house at 149 Cedar St."

"One moment. I'll see if he's available."

After a moment of silence, Mayor Jonathon Thompson said, "This is Mayor Jonathon. What can I do for you, Jeff?"

"Well, you could've left my house alone, but it's too late for that," Jeff said into his phone, clutched in one gloved hand.

On the other end of the line, Jonathon sighed. "Jeff, we've been over this a hundred times already. Frankly, I don't know why I even took your call." His voice was cool, detached. Jeff squeezed the cell phone to his ear; the mayor's professional tone of voice was as aggravating as ever. "I guess I keep hoping you'll come to your senses and get over it. Accept it; this is how it's going to be. Now please, let the rest of our conversations be through our attorneys. They'll work this out."

"I only wanted to live in peace," Jeff responded. "I wanted to be proud of my home, take care of my wife, and live in peace. Don't you understand, Jonathon? You took that from me. Now I can never get it back." He hit "end" and let the phone fall.

Jeff needed to make that call. He needed to know Jonathon was in his office. He needed to know he hadn't planned all this in vain. After going through all this trouble, he'd get his reward.

The phone landed on the floor beside the accelerator, as Jeff stepped on the gas and rocketed through the parking lot. At nine in the morning, the Thursday before Christmas 2011, few citizens visited city hall. Jeff lucked out: fewer barriers between his Toyota Matrix and what he intended to do.

City hall lay straight ahead.

The glass and steel double doors opened from within, and a woman stepped out. She dashed out of the way just as she'd seen Jeff's car and, in the split second before he hit the building, realizing he wasn't stopping. Jeff didn't know whether she made it to safety or not. It didn't matter as the glass came shattering down over the roof of the car and steel scraped the doors with an agonized groan. After the first set of doors, Jeff hit the second set.

Jeff rocked forward in his seat before his seatbelt arrested his momentum. He felt the jolt as his seatbelt tightened and the airbag deployed, slamming into his chest and face. It stung him as it threw his arms clear of the steering wheel. His head slammed into the headrest. His body rocked with the shock wave, but Jeff had no intention of letting the doors slow him down. He floored the gas. The car lurched forward from the wreckage.

It was almost beautiful, like the Fourth of July, the way sparks flew and glass shattered. With the noise of steel scraping against steel, Jeff's entrance put the town's annual fireworks display to shame. Jeff inhaled and the smell of the gas can in the back seat hit his nose. He hoped the sparks wouldn't start the fire yet.

The door's steel supports twisted upward with the impact, colliding with the ceiling. In an enormous cloud of dust, white textured ceiling panels and light fixtures cascaded to the floor. Wires snapped and sparked.

The door handle hit the driver's side window. The glass cracked, then splintered into the small shards raining down on Jeff. The handle pulled free from what remained of the door, falling into the car as it struck Jeff. Something wet ran down his cheek, and Jeff knew he'd caught at least one of the fragments with his face. He blinked at the pain, then forgot it.

Jeff barely had time to be amazed he'd made it as he barreled down the hallway, determined to reach the mayor's office. Clearing the destruction, Jeff saw a flash of the face of the plumbing inspector in the split second before his body went down under the wheels of Jeff's car.

Jeff looked in the rear-view mirror; the plumbing inspector lay dying in the hallway, a pool of blood collecting under his head. The recognition of what he'd done hit Jeff, leaving an aching feeling in the pit of his stomach. Jeff determined when he decided to hit the gas pedal he would act as a soldier. He knew there was the possibility of collateral damage, that people who weren't involved could be victims.

"Damn it!" Jeff said to himself. "I was starting to like that guy."

"He's got a gun!" a woman shouted. The car shot past four more stunned onlookers. Jeff recognized one of them. Though he currently served as the head of Code Enforcement, Earl McGhee had been a police officer in his day. Jeff wasn't surprised Earl was still packing. Because of the number of people in the hall, Earl didn't have a clear shot. If he had, Jeff knew he'd already be dead, or at least mortally wounded.

Instead, Earl's single shot hit the windshield, already shattered to tiny pieces. The bullet pierced the plastic barrier and entered the car, narrowly missing Jeff. Jeff flinched as the shattered glass tumbled in.

"Stop right there, Jeff!" Earl shouted. Everyone in city hall knew Jeff after his long battle. They probably weren't even surprised to see Jeff's car barreling down the halls.

At the end of a long hall lined with half-light office doors sat Mayor Jonathon Thompson's office. Stunned workers poured out of those doors. Some ran for their lives, while others stared in a daze at the wreckage and the speeding car as it slid sideways to a halt in front of the wooden doors to the mayor's office. As he exited the car, he took a Zippo from his coat pocket, lit the flame and let it drop to the passenger seat. Jeff hoped the burning car would force everyone out of the building…and block the mayor's escape.

He'd considered using a bottle bomb to blow the car to hell. He'd learned the technique online. Supposedly, you had about an hour between making the bomb and the time the explosives would eat their way into the aluminum, triggering the chemical reaction. But Jeff had other work to finish before he reached city hall. He decided he couldn't risk an explosion on his drive between destinations. In the end he decided a simple can of gas would do the job as well, without the risks.

Jeff had blocked the mayor's primary exit; now the only way in or out was through the receptionist's office. He turned his head for a split second and noticed the tire tracks lining the hall, stained with blood, before he entered the receptionist's office and slammed the door shut behind him.

Once inside, he pushed over a short file cabinet. He knew Earl lurked out there with a gun and might burst in before the fire burned out of control. Jeff wanted to keep the smoke and flames out of the mayor's office as long as possible. He feared for his life, but even more, he knew it was time to complete his mission.

The mayor's secretary, Rachelle, still sat behind her desk in the midst of the chaos. Jeff remembered she'd been friendly with him, even sympathetic. Jeff didn't need her mixed up in this mess.

"Leave," Jeff shouted at Rachelle, taking the sawed off shotgun from inside his jacket. She hesitated, looking toward the door to the mayor's inner office. "Now. I said now!"

Rachelle got up from behind her desk and ran into the office behind her, the city clerk's office. The clerk's office provided another exit. He exhaled, grateful to have given Rachelle her chance to escape as he forced open the door to Mayor Jonathon's inner office.

The mayor stood, leaning over his desk. "Put the gun away, Jeff. This doesn't have to end like this."

Mayor Jonathon Thompson, in his late thirties, looked much younger than Jeff's forty-four years. He had what Jeff considered a "baby face." Fat when he'd been elected, after eight years in office he'd probably put on another hundred pounds, and it showed in his cheeks and jowls. His pale blond hair didn't help him look any older or thinner. All together, his face gave the impression of an oversized, grossly overfed infant. The starched collar of his blue shirt cut into his fat neck. Jeff could see the sweat already drenching Jonathon.

Jeff's hatred of Jonathon boiled to the surface again, as it had during the phone call. As it had, in fact, during every one of the phone calls between these two men since the day

Jeff learned the town intended to turn his property into a sidewalk.

"Shut up," Jeff sneered. "I'm tired of your bullshit, Jonathon. You've been trying to smooth-talk your way through this as you lie to and manipulate the citizens of this city for your own purposes. I'm going to put an end to all that. Sit down, Jonathon. You get up again and I'll just fucking shoot you." He kicked a tall trash can over, barring the door. It wasn't enough, though, and Jeff immediately began stacking everything he could get his hands on around and on top of it.

"Okay, okay," Jonathon said, as cool as ever as he sat down behind his desk. He placed his hands on top of the desk, palms down, where Jeff could see them. Jeff was irritated at Jonathon's falsely calm demeanor, but glad he had the sense to keep his hands in plain sight.

Jeff paced back and forth in the small amount of space the office allowed him. He expected Earl to burst through the door at any moment with his police buddies, guns blazing. Jeff knew he'd likely die at the outcome of this, but that didn't mean he was eager to catch a bullet.

"I understand your rage," Jonathon continued. "I'd be enraged, too, if some son-of-a-bitch politician told me he was going to take my house for a civic project."

Civic project: Jonathon was fucking joking. This battle had long ago stopped being about the town's right to build a river walkway connecting Central Park with Silver Park. This was about Jonathon Thompson's attempt to make the town his own personal legacy, and the citizens be damned. Jeff learned long ago the mayor didn't like the way he and Kendra were renovating the house. Jonathon personally wanted the house torn down; he'd all but told Jeff so himself. This was personal now.

"You don't understand anything," Jeff returned, brandishing the gun. "You're not going to smooth-talk your way out of this, Thompson. The most dangerous man in the world is the man who has nothing left to lose. You took away everything that meant something to me. What else do I have to lose?"

As he spoke, the mayor's hands slipped under the desk. Jeff reacted without thinking, squeezing the trigger. The blast struck Jonathon, annihilating his left arm. Blood flew in all directions, splattering the file cabinet behind Jonathon and the papers on his desk.

Jeff thought about how happy it made him to finally see the mayor bleeding and suffering. Jonathon had no idea of the suffering he'd caused for Jeff and Kendra. Now it was Jeff's turn to watch Jonathon twitch in pain. It felt almost redeeming, somehow.

Five minutes had passed since Jeff had gotten into the mayor's office, and the temperature soared. From the sounds of the alarm and the fire trucks wailing outside, the rest of the building still burned. Jeff could smell the acrid smoke pouring in through the crack under the doors.

Good, Jeff thought as he grabbed the blanket from the back of the mayor's sofa and stuffed it under the doorway to hold back the smoke. No one would come through his barricades and get to him now...except maybe the fire department with a battering ram. Everything would be over for Jeff before that happened.

"What do you want? What do you want?" Jonathon pleaded. "I'll give you anything."

"Yeah? What are you going to give me, asshole? What is your life worth? Half a million? A million? Two million? Tell me, what is your life worth?" He stuck his shotgun barrel against Jonathon's head and screamed, "Tell me, you piece of shit: what is your life worth?"

Jonathon said, "I can't tell you. It's priceless."

"Yeah, well, so was my liberty, you fuckin' shit," Jeff said as he stepped back and let his gun down.

From outside, a woman's voice shrieked through the glass, "You bastard!"

The windows rattled behind closed blinds as the enraged woman beat on them with both fists. "You killed my daughter!" she screamed.

Jeff jumped at the sound. He and Jonathon stared into one another's eyes. He said to Jonathon, "Look and see who that is."

Jonathon turned and peered through the blinds. "It's Erin Clarke," he said.

"Tell her to go away," Jeff growled at the mayor.

Jonathon flinched, wincing in pain as he held his wounded arm. "If I move, you'll shoot me. You tell her."

"I'll shoot you if you don't tell her, you stupid asshole."

In the hall, Jeff heard the firefighters. He heard the force of the water as they turned their hoses on the burning car. Water, tainted by soot, rushed under the door and soaked the carpet of the mayor's office.

On the other side of the window, Erin pounded, still screaming, "You killed my daughter!"

Jeff realized what he'd done. He said to the mayor, "Tell her to go away."

Jonathon yelled, "Erin! Erin, can you hear me?"

She stopped pounding for a moment. "Jonathon? Are you all right?"

"Don't worry about me. I'm fine." His words sounded illogical as he held his bleeding, mangled arm, which oozed dark blood onto the once-blue sleeve of his shirt. "You need to go or he'll kill me."

Jeff fired his shotgun at the ceiling and shouted, "Get out of here! I'm not fucking around!" A cloud of dust and crumbled ceiling tile rained down on him.

Three - Home Owners
March, 2002

Sometimes, Jeff still couldn't believe this girl wanted to hang out with him, much less marry him. At twenty-four and nearly ten years younger than him, Kendra Wilson gave Jeff everything he could ask for. Her parents had invested in sending her to a private, all-woman, liberal arts college, where Kendra majored in business. After graduation, she'd gone on to complete a computer programming course and landed a job as a layout designer for a local magazine, the River Rock. It didn't exactly pay the bills, but Kendra did her job with talent and enthusiasm.

Kendra's chocolate-brown hair fell down to her collarbone. The old saying 'gentlemen prefer blondes' didn't apply to Jeff. He preferred the "girl next door" look, and Kendra had it. With her small, delicate features and wide blue eyes, she drew looks wherever she and Jeff went. She rarely wore make-up, and looked all the better because of it. She kept herself in shape, taking time every morning before work to do sit-ups and walk on the treadmill. She had curves in all the right places.

Now Jeff and Kendra had a chance to show the house of their dreams to Kendra's parents. Their real estate agent Margot let them in, then left them alone while she met with another client in Willow Bend. Kendra's mother, Candace, walked around the house with her eyes wide. Jeff asked her what she thought.

"It's so big! I love it. I would love to live here myself. Of course, it's a lot of work," she said in an anxious tone.

"Don't forget, I've owned a lot of houses," Jeff told her and Kendra's father, Wade. Wade hadn't said much of anything the whole time they'd been touring the place. "I know how things are supposed to be done. I'm going to be a really aggressive buyer, and Kendra and I are going to end up with a whole lot more than we're going to pay for."

"I hope so," Candace said, sighing. "This place really could be beautiful with a lot of TLC."

"You're damn right it could," Jeff agreed. "Don't forget, this is riverfront property. When I rented that apartment on the lake, I saw tiny bungalows sell for a hundred to a hundred and fifty thousand dollars. The new owners tore them down and build mini-mansions worth anywhere from half a million to a million dollars. That's the life cycle of waterfront property: it gets harder to own as people build bigger, grander, and more exclusive neighborhoods. Nothing increases in value like waterfront property. It's getting to the point where unless you're rich, you can't live on the water anymore. They're pricing waterfront property so high these days, ordinary people can't have it. I really think if I do this right, it'll be the deal of a lifetime. The most valuable thing we'll ever own; by the time we're old and gray, we'll be able to sell this place for at least half a million dollars. This house will be our retirement some day."

"It's so big," Candace repeated. "What do you need all this space for?"

Wade ignored her. "I believe you can do it," he told Jeff proudly. "I believe you two can do anything you set your minds to." His opinion made Jeff proud.

149 North Cedar Street needed a lot of work. Despite its flaws, though, it had many charms. It stood alone, with the Cedar Street bridge literally coming to an end in its front yard. A haggard, half-dead maple tree stood in front. At the other end of the yard, a low wall separated the property from the flower shop's parking lot. The house had two stories, with white siding and a steep, green roof in obvious need of repair. A large gable covered all four sides of the house, with long valleys that stopped just above the first floor windows. The wooden arbor needed some work, its white paint peeled, but underneath the wood seemed in good shape. Its whimsical curves gave the house a distinctive entry way, even if the exterior storm door, clear glass from top to bottom, did make the front room seem like an aquarium. Through the front room, a set of old-style French doors led into a smaller side room lined with windows on two sides. The river gleamed

through both sides. The first time she'd seen it, Kendra had remarked, "This would make a perfect office. I could sit here and work on the magazine while I stare out at the water. Doesn't it look peaceful?"

As they lay in bed in their loft in Willow Bend, Jeff said to Kendra, "How much would you love to live near the river in Princess City?"

Their wedding date approached, and Jeff and Kendra discussed getting out of the apartment. As much as they liked the loft, they couldn't make economic sense of continuing to pay rent on it every month when they could put the same money into a house payment and earning some equity. Jeff liked the sound of equity, the sound of actually owning something that would be his and Kendra's.

"We live on the same river now," she said, turning over on her pillow. "Only further north." In fact, if they'd listened closely, from their beds they could hear the rushing sounds of the raceway rejoining the river at the end of the island.

"But we don't own this place. If we put a bid on the house on Cedar, we could actually own a piece of river-front property."

"I would like to have our own river bank," Kendra said.

"We could water-ski on this part of the river, too. It's flat, not choppy like our part of the river. We could get a boat. Not only that, but it's close to the parks. I can fish in Central

Park, and we can use the tennis courts in the summer. A few blocks in the other direction and we'd be at Silver Park. We can swim in the summer and ice skate in the winter. And no more sharing walls with our neighbors. In fact, no neighbors! You can play the stereo as loud as you want, and no one will say a thing."

"You make it sound like it's out in the middle of nowhere. It's as much downtown as the loft. In fact, I think when I looked out that second floor window on the south side, I could see the red roof of the Wellington Mansion."

The Wellington Mansion, once the home of Princess City's wealthy rubber plant owners, developed into an elegant bed and breakfast. The River Rock held its Christmas parties there, though Kendra, hired months before, hadn't attended one yet.

"I'm sure you did. That's the real beauty of this house: it's hidden in plain sight, near the main road through town but separated from it by the bridge, inaccessible from the river side, and still easy for your family to get to. It would be our own little urban oasis."

"Only not so little," she countered. "It needs a lot of work before we can have people over."

"A lot of work," he agreed, "but it's what I do. Do you think I'm good at my job, Kendra?"

"Yeah, of course you are."

"If I'm that way on other people's houses, imagine how hard I'm going to work on my own home. I've moved a lot more than you have in my life, and I've always believed that every time I left a place, I left it in better shape than when I moved in. This Cedar Street house may look run down, but it will be a palace when I'm done with it."

"My own little Taj Mahal," Kendra laughed, and Jeff laughed along with her.

"I don't know about that," Jeff said. "I doubt it's going to get that fancy."

"No, I mean it will be your labor of love. The Taj Mahal was built for a woman by a man who was in love," she said.

He continued, "The only thing that worries me is the way those joists sagged on the second floor. Before we put in an offer on it, we'll have to get a structural engineer to look at the place, make sure it doesn't need some kind of major repairs."

"Are you really sure you want to commit yourself to a rehab this major?"

"I'm sure if you're sure," Jeff said. "We'll keep looking, of course, but if we decide that's the house we want, then that's the house we'll get. You're not afraid of a little hard work, are you?"

Kendra pulled the covers over her head. "Yes, I am," she said. "I'm very, very afraid."

He pulled the covers over his own head, sealing them both under the blankets and sheets, and pulled Kendra to him. "I'm really going to need your help on this, Kendra. Even though I'm the one who has the remodeling expertise and the home-buying experience, there's no way I can pull off something like this alone."

"I know," she said. "Jeff, I'll be right here to help you with whatever you need."

"You'd better be," he said teasingly, holding her hand and paying special attention to her engagement ring.

Jeff personally inspected the house from attic to basement, then had a meeting with a structural engineer. Over dinner that night, Jeff explained to Kendra what he'd found out about the house. "Is the structural damage bad?" she asked.

"It's nothing that would make the house unlivable, but the engineer thinks it's probably about $15,000 worth of repairs to correct everything. We'll know the exact number in a few days, when we get the engineer's report."

She spooned another helping of green beans onto her plate. "Then we'll get Margot to call the seller's agent and ask him to take $15,000 off the asking price."

"That's not how it works. Typically, we'd spilt the cost. Since our offer at $75,000 has already been accepted contingent upon the inspections, we would take off half of the $15,000, which would be $7500, and our new offer would be $67,500."

"Could they really be willing to go that low?"

"By law, after the place has been inspected, the seller has to disclose all the findings to every potential buyer. He can't hide these things, so nobody else is going to want this place. That's how it works."

"I'm glad you understand all of this," Kendra said, sounding mystified.

"Are you sure this is what we want to do?" Jeff asked her. "I know we were looking for a handyman's special, but these problems are serious. The house might be ready to fall apart."

Kendra thought for a moment, then said, "Jeff, I think I love that house."

"Should I be jealous?"

"I'm serious, Jeff. I've been thinking about what you said to Mom and Dad about waterfront property, and despite all of its problems, it's in a great location. We haven't seen anything better, Jeff. Let's make that offer to the seller's agent. I want this house."

Jeff still had his doubts, but he could overlook them to make Kendra happy. He would've done anything to make her happy.

The seller's agent balked at the structural engineer's estimate. For the next week, Margot and Jeff battled it out with the seller's agent while Kendra worked, listening from the sidelines. In the end, the seller and Margot agreed buyer and seller would split the difference on the repair costs. Jeff was right; they got it for the $67,500.

As he tried to sleep, Jeff wondered if he and Kendra had made a mistake signing the contract and agreeing to absorb some of the costs of those structural repairs. He asked himself if in his determination to make Kendra happy, he'd talked himself into doing something stupid. He had to face facts: she might be "in love" with this house, but at twenty-four years old, she'd never bought a house before. She'd never even lived away from her parents, except in the loft and her college dorms. He was the one with all the real estate experience; if this deal soured, everyone would blame him. Jeff couldn't sleep; signing the contract had given him severe buyer's remorse.

Four - Home Sweet Home
March 2002

Jeff and Kendra lay in bed, exhausted but happy after making love. She didn't go into the office until noon on Fridays, and they hesitated to get up and get dressed. They both groaned as the phone rang.

"Don't answer it," Kendra said. "Let 'em leave a message."

He considered it, but on the next ring, he said, "It could be a customer." Jeff had an expression when the phone rang: "That's the sound of money, either coming in or going out."

He went around the corner to the living room and took the phone off the coffee table. "Hello?"

"Hello. Jeff, this is Sal Marino from the credit union. The board and I have come to a decision on your financing."

"You have?"

"Yes. We've decided to go ahead and let the financing go through, on the condition that you get the house rezoned."

"Rezoned? What are you talking about?"

Sal said, "The house is zoned commercial, because the previous owner used it as a rental property, right? We need you to get it rezoned residential. Our credit union doesn't finance commercial properties."

"That's no problem," Jeff said. "We don't need it as a commercial property anyway. Thanks, Sal." He hung up.

Jeff was surprised to see Kendra standing there, wearing Jeff's undershirt and nothing else. "Was it a customer?" she asked.

"No, it was the credit union. We have to have the house rezoned. They'll only finance a residential property. I'll have to call Margot and see who she knows to get it taken care of. She and her husband are big wigs with the local Republican Party; I'm sure they can expedite it."

Jeff called Margot. He left a message on her voice mail, but she called him shortly after Jeff and Kendra got dressed. He explained the rezoning situation to her.

"I'll make a few phone calls and get back with you," Margot said.

She called back later that afternoon, while Jeff worked in the garage. "I talked with Elizabeth Montoya," Margot said. "She's a member of the town council. She says the docket is full for the next two meetings; they meet every two weeks. She'll make sure it's on the docket three meetings from now, though, so in a month in a half you'll be able to get it rezoned."

"But we're supposed to close in two weeks."

"I'm sorry, Jeff. That's the best news I can give you right now."

Jeff called Sal back. "It's going to be a month and a half before I can have my house rezoned, Sal. I have to wait for the next town council meeting that doesn't already have a full docket. The seller isn't going to rezone it for us. He's afraid he'll be stuck with a residential property if the sale doesn't go through, and he doesn't want that. He's convinced the house has more value as a commercial property."

"I'll tell you what, Jeff: you give me your word you'll get the house rezoned, and we'll still go through with the closing on good faith. I've known Kendra since before she was born, literally. Candace and Wade Wilson have been coming to my credit union since they were newlyweds. I trust you, Jeff. And if I find out I can't trust you, I know where to find you." He laughed; Jeff laughed along.

Jeff called Margot again; this time she picked right up. "The closing date is still on," he said.

"Good, because I'm tired of working on this piece of shit house," Margot said. Jeff could understand where she was coming from; she was losing money every time the price of the property went down.

Anxiety prevailed for the next two weeks. Jeff and Kendra had the house appraised. The appraiser told Jeff, "I wouldn't buy this house," as he sat down on the couch left behind by the previous owner. Jeff and Kendra went up and down on an emotional roller coaster between elation and regret.

Two weeks later, at the closing meeting, the credit union loaned Kendra and Jeff eighty percent of the house's $125,000 appraised value, $100,000. Minus the $67,500 they paid for the house and closing costs, they had a check for $32,500. They went immediately from the meeting room to the teller line with their check and deposited it in their joint checking account. As they sat in the van, Kendra stared at the receipt.

"I've never seen this much money before in my life," she said. "Have you?"

"Don't forget, I've bought houses before," he said. "But, no, not this much."

"Well, I haven't either. I've never held anything that had this many zeroes before. I can't believe you did this. I'm not sure I even understand how you did this, but I can't believe you did!"

"We did this," Jeff corrected her. "Don't forget, Kendra, this is a team effort. I couldn't have done any of this without you."

*****

About thirty citizens filled the folding chairs in front of the long table as Jeff went to have his house rezoned. A city council member read from a list of items up for discussion; the house on Cedar Street appeared ninth on the docket. Jeff waited to hear the chairman say, "Next item: should the house at 149 North Cedar Street be rezoned R-1, residential?"

Jeff stood up looking unsure of what to do. "Come up here to the microphone and explain your side of things."

Jeff didn't expect to have to speak much. He'd assumed the town council would already have all the facts in front of them. He stepped up the microphone sitting on a short stand on top of a lectern. He said, "I need to have my house rezoned."

"Why?" one of the council members asked.

"Because the credit union says so," Jeff explained. "It's considered a commercial property now, but I'd like to have it rezoned R-2, so my fiancée and I could still rent out the upstairs."

The council member at the end of the table looked interested. She was in her early 60s, though her stark-white hair stood out. She wore diamond stud earrings and a conservative tan jacket over a white blouse. "What is your name, sir?"

"Jeffrey Gray. My fiancée, Kendra Wilson, and I are the purchasers of this house. Kendra couldn't be here with me tonight. She's working late."

"Mr. Gray," the council member continued, "My name is Elizabeth Montoya. Not only do I represent District Four, in which 149 North Cedar Street is located, but I also live on Edgewater Drive, practically right across the street from you. I've been seeing improvements to the house on Cedar. Have you been doing those yourself?"

"Yes," Jeff said. "I'm a professional remodeler, and I plan to restore the property as well as live in it."

"I'm glad you're going to live there yourself," she said. "When it was a rental property, it attracted certain undesirables. I'm glad to see the place going into the hands of a professional who knows what he's doing with it."

"Thank you," Jeff said.

Elizabeth continued, "So, if you and your fiancée are going to live in the property, why are you asking the council to rezone it R-2 instead of R-1?"

Jeff considered his answer; he didn't want to give the council, and the whole town, the impression he had no business living in this neighborhood. He didn't want them to think he and Kendra couldn't afford to live there. "For a little extra income."

The council discussed the matter among themselves. In the end, the chairman told Jeff, "We don't like the idea of rezoning you R-2. We'd rather have a single family who cares about the place than another group of renters who come and go.

We'd hate to see the property deteriorate again. We've decided to rezone the home R-1, single family only."

Jeff was disappointed. The council was telling him he wouldn't be allowed to rent out the apartment now, losing Jeff and Kendra an extra six or seven hundred dollars every month. He'd hoped to have some extra rental income.

After the meeting, Elizabeth came up to Jeff. "You say you're a professional remodeler? My husband and I have been looking for someone to redo our bathroom. We have a custom ceramic shower that needs new grout, and I've been thinking of switching over from our plain white tiles to something more colorful. In fact, I might have the whole shower redone. Is that something you do?"

"Absolutely," Jeff said. He handed Elizabeth one of his cards.

"Oh, and we had our back porch enclosed and made into a three-season room last summer, but we didn't have the windows painted at the time, and now I'm sorry we didn't. Do you paint windows?"

"Painting was my first specialty before I branched out into general contracting."

"I'd rather have it done by someone local," she added. "I suppose I can't get much more local than my new neighbor down the street!"

The possibilities of working for one of the town council members excited Jeff, but losing the rental income still disappointed him. He had to relay the bad news to Kendra when she got home from work.

"What does this mean?" Kendra asked him, sounding anxious.

"We're not going to have a tenant," he replied. "We're going to have to work extra hard, Kendra, because not only will we have to make all of the improvements to the house, but we'll also have to keep plugging away at our day jobs so we can afford to come up with the mortgage payments on our own every month. Our savings account isn't going to get filled up very fast."

Kendra looked worried, as she always did when he took this serious tone of voice. "We'll figure it out, I guess," she said, but she didn't sound sure. Like her mother, Kendra worried. Her parents had done everything for her. Jeff knew exactly what Kendra was thinking: she didn't know how she was going to cope with this kind of responsibility.

"We always do," Jeff responded. "We've known each other for two years now, and in all that time, have I ever let you down when you and I needed something?"

"No," she admitted. "You always find a way to come up with it."

"This won't be any different," he said. "We're just going to have to work hard." Jeff sensed he was going to have to push Kendra to get some of that hard work out of her. He only hoped he would be able to cope with her inexperience and worry.

*****

Jeff could've been a professional mover; he'd done it enough times. Being a landlord and having to make hasty evictions had only sharpened his skills. Kendra watched in awe as he threw virtually everything in the bedroom other than the TV onto the middle of the bedspread, bundled it up, and headed to the van. Lex and Jeff had moved all of the heavy furniture over the weekend. Lex, short for Alexander, was Kendra's brother, two years younger. He had worked for Jeff part-time.

Elizabeth Montoya had called Jeff the previous morning to tell him she'd accepted his remodeling bid, so Jeff hired Lex as his full-time assistant. Now Lex would get an hourly salary whether the two of them worked on Elizabeth's or on Jeff's. Both projects needed plenty of work done.

When Jeff returned, Kendra was still loading her books into a plastic tub, one by one. "You can't put all the books together," Jeff advised her. "You'll never be able to lift that thing. Fill it halfway with books and the other half with the throw pillows from the couch."

Under Jeff's direction, they had the loft packed and loaded into the van, and Wade Wilson's pickup truck, in no time. While Wade and Jeff drove the vehicles over to the new house, Kendra stayed behind with a basket of paper towels and cleaning supplies.

Jeff and Wade returned to a spic-and-span apartment. Jeff inspected the kitchen and bathroom to make sure Kendra hadn't forgotten to clean behind the toilet and around the refrigerator seal. Everything looked good, so he went back into the living room and gave her a big hug.

"It's strange to see this place without any furniture," Kendra said. "It seems like we were just moving in here."

"Don't worry," her father said. "It will be a long, long time before you have to go through this again. You'll probably live in the new house for the rest of your lives."

"I hope so," Jeff said. "That house, and all the equity we're going to build in it, is supposed to be my retirement."

"Our retirement," Kendra reminded him.

That first day, Jeff, Kendra, and Wade stacked most of the boxes in a back living room of the house. Jeff had already torn the mutilated ceilings the rest of the way down, and Lex had cleaned up the debris. The two living rooms became a storage area. Jeff and Kendra set up a bedroom/living room in one of the upstairs bedrooms. The rest of the house resembled a construction zone more than living space, but this one room was nearly perfect.

After Wade left that evening, Jeff and Kendra ordered a spinach-Alfredo pizza from Mario's, a Princess City restaurant they'd never tried before. They washed their pizza down with a celebratory bottle of wine before they spent their first night in the house.

The next day, Lex showed up late for work and put Jeff in a foul mood. "I had to stop for cigarettes," he explained.

"How did it take you half an hour to buy a pack of cigarettes?" Jeff wondered out loud. Lex didn't answer him, and Jeff let the matter drop.

They went to Elizabeth's, though Elizabeth had already left for her job at the bank. Her retired husband, Carl, would supervise their work. "Not that I'm going to hover," Carl insisted. "I'll be here to let you in, though." He showed them which windows they were to paint from the three-season room, then disappeared into his office in the back of the house with a tall coffee and the Wall Street Journal.

Carl, Jeff discovered, sat at his computer much of the day, trading stocks. Money didn't seem like much of an issue for the couple. The Montoya house wasn't the largest or the newest on Edgewater Drive, but the inside of the two-story brick home looked like the pages of an architectural digest.

The guest bath exuded luxury. The dullest thing about it was the all-white ceramic shower. Jeff and Lex saw the tile Elizabeth wanted to use to replace it; the thick, deep-green tiles reminded Jeff of the bottom of an old bottle.

"Cool," Lex said as he turned over the sample tile on the edge of the sink.

"Be careful with that," Jeff said. "You don't want to scratch that sink, and you really don't want to drop that thing on your toes."

Jeff and Lex disassembled the shower doors and stored the pieces in the garage, out of Carl and Elizabeth's way. Then Jeff gave Lex the sledgehammer and put him in charge of knocking down the old tiles while Jeff removed the windows in the three-season room.

On day two, when they had the old shower completely demolished, Jeff set up a workshop in his basement where Lex could paint the window sashes. He left Lex there. He went down the street to the Montoya's, where he mixed concrete to pour and shape the foundation for the new shower pan.

That evening, Jeff received an anxious phone call from Elizabeth. "Jeff, how long were you at my house today?" she asked.

"A couple of hours," Jeff said. "Is there a problem?"

He could hear the frustration in Elizabeth's voice. "Not with your work, per se. I was hoping you were going to spend longer days at my house, though. I thought we were trying to have my bathroom put back together as soon as possible."

"I am. I poured concrete today; there isn't even anything else I can do until the concrete dries."

"How long does concrete take to dry?" she asked. "Because I'm looking at it and it looks dry already. Are you going to come back over here? It's only four in the afternoon."

Jeff didn't care about the time; he made his own work hours, and they didn't go by the clock. He didn't want to risk offending Elizabeth, though. "Elizabeth, I've done everything I can to your home today. This isn't the first shower base I've ever poured. This is how it's done."

Elizabeth seemed to think that over for a moment before she responded, "What about my windows? You could at least be over here working on my windows."

"My brother-in-law is working on your windows. He put the first coat of paint on them this morning, and we're waiting for those to dry, too."

"I thought you would be further by now," Elizabeth huffed.

You thought wrong, Jeff thought, but he didn't say it. Instead he said, "Elizabeth, my helper and I will do our best to have your bathroom and your three-season room done, in a professional manner, as soon as is practical. We're going to be there for at least two to three weeks, so please, be patient. I'm sure I told you before I got started that the job was going to take that long."

"Okay," she said, though she didn't sound convinced.

On Friday, Elizabeth had gone to work when Jeff and Lex showed up. Carl greeted them at the door, saying, "I heard my wife wasn't too happy with you the other night."

"She wanted this job done yesterday," Jeff replied.

"She's like that," Carl said. "Elizabeth isn't a very patient person."

I wish I'd known that before I agreed to work for her, Jeff thought. He always imagined himself as a mirror. When people were sweet, kind and smiling to him, he was sweet, kind and smiling right back. When someone got ugly with him, though, he showed them an ugly reflection. Jeff preferred to work with mellow customers. He knew he did good work and that he would see it through to the end; he expected his customers to take him at his word when he told them so. Elizabeth's phone call had gotten under his skin.

Later that day, as Jeff and Lex cleaned up to go for a lunch break. Carl wandered over from his office, still clutching his Wall Street Journal.

"We'll be back in about an hour," Jeff told Carl.

Carl raised his eyebrows. "Is Elizabeth going to be happy with your progress when she gets home from the bank?"

Elizabeth riding his back was bad enough; now Carl wanted in on giving Jeff some shit. "You know, Carl, one time I did a painting job for a woman who kept nagging me about how I was doing things and when I was going to get it done. You know what I did? I went to my bank and got every bit of the money she'd given me. Even though I was half way through the job, I gave her a full refund and told her to go to hell."

Carl didn't say anything, but that night, Jeff got another call from Elizabeth. "I'm sorry," she said. "I've been a bad customer."

"No, you haven't," Jeff assured her. "You've been a little impatient, that's all."

Despite Elizabeth's apology, Jeff called Lex that evening and told him, "I know I said we'd take the weekend off, but I want to get that shower tiled as quickly as possible now that we've got the base set. I really need your help tomorrow."

"The thing about tomorrow is, there's this party I'm planning on going to tonight. I've been looking forward to it for more than a week now, and I have a feeling I'm going to be pretty trashed by the end of this thing. You know how it is…I'm not really going to feel like working on Saturday. It wouldn't be fair to you; I wouldn't be at my best," Lex said

"So don't go to the party," Jeff countered. "You're working for a manager's salary, even though you're an assistant with no experience. Elizabeth is going to drive me crazy if I have to work on her shower too much longer, Lex. Let's get this thing over with. I really need you this Saturday."

To Jeff's surprise, Lex started to cry. "I wanted to go to this party," he said, sounding like a frustrated toddler.

"You're an adult now, Lex. Sometimes you have to do things you don't really want to do. It's good for you, though. Makes you a better person when you can commit to something and stick with it, even when the going gets rough." Or even when the going gets mildly unpleasant, Jeff thought, marveling at what a big baby his brother-in-law sounded like. "Now, are you going to work with me, or not?"

"I'll be there," Lex said. He might as well have added, "But I won't like it."

On Saturday morning, around nine, Jeff called Lex's cell phone to ask Lex where he was. Lex didn't answer, so Jeff left a voice mail message. "Call me as soon as you get this," Jeff said. "I'm going down to Elizabeth's now; you can meet me there." He called Lex's house phone and left the same message on it. Then he went to work, installing shower tiles. He mixed a bucket of mortar and started tiling.

Jeff looked down at his watch; it was already noon, and Lex hadn't called him back yet. He picked up his cell phone and dialed Lex again.

This time, Lex picked up. "Hello?" He sounded as if he'd just gotten out of bed. Maybe he was still in bed, for all Jeff knew.

"Lex, what time are you coming to work? It's noon already, and I left you a message three hours ago."

"I'm not working today," Lex admitted. "I feel like shit. I drank way too much last night."

Jeff seethed. He'd told Lex not to go to that damn party, and it sounded like Lex understood his point of view, even if he had been disappointed. "You went to that party, didn't you?"

"I told you, I was looking forward to it for more than a week. I couldn't not go."

"You could've not gotten trashed," Jeff said through his teeth, frustration seeping into his voice. "I told you I needed you today, man. Did you not take me seriously? I mean, how could you do this to me, Lex?"

Lex started to cry again. "I didn't do anything to you, Jeff. Stop yelling at me; I told you I was sick today. I'll call you tomorrow, okay?"

Jeff hung up the phone. "That asshole," he said to himself. "How can he be such a selfish shit?" Glad Kendra wasn't around to hear him ranting about her brother, he also wished she could understand what her brother acted like when she wasn't around.

Jeff finished as many tiles as he could by himself. When Kendra came home from some wedding-related field trip with her mother, she called Jeff to see if he needed anything. He told her about Lex flaking out on him, and Kendra offered to put on a pair of work jeans and an old t-shirt and come over to help.

When she arrived, Jeff looked at Kendra with her faded jeans with the hole in one knee and her ripped Smashing Pumpkins t-shirt, the one she'd snuck from Lex's laundry basket while they were still in high school. "If I would've known I was coming over to a house this fancy, I would've dressed up a little," she joked. "I feel weird being in someone else's house when they're not here." Elizabeth and Carl had gone to the Farmer's Market.

"Oh, get over it," Jeff told her. "This is my job; I do this every day."

She changed her tune, however, once Jeff handed her the grout brush and bucket of water and gave her the task of cleaning the tiles as he set them. She soon learned how much work went into making straight, clean grout lines in a shower...and how much mortar ended up on the person doing the scrubbing. "I can't believe Lex didn't show up," she said as she scrubbed.

"Why not? It's typical Lex, if you think about it. You practically have to pull teeth from him to get him involved in anything for the family anyway, and then when you do, he'll take any excuse to get out of it. Granted, when he's here, he helps me out a lot. I wish it wasn't such a struggle to get him to want to be here, though. Wasn't he like that when you were growing up?"

"I guess so," Kendra said. "I guess I've been willing to forgive a lot because he's my brother and I love him."

"I love him, too," Jeff added, "but that doesn't mean I'm always going to be willing to put up with his shit. Lex can only push me so far, and then he's going to find out I push back."

"Fair enough," Kendra said, bending to wipe a splotch of mortar off the top of her shoe. The whitish mortar looked like toothpaste.

Working together, Jeff and Kendra managed to finish putting up most of the full-sized shower tiles. Only the cut pieces and the tapered bull nose tiles around the outside edges remained.

On Monday morning, Lex called Jeff and told him he'd be there for work at nine.

"It's already nine-twenty," Jeff pointed out.

"Shit," Lex said. "I still need to take a shower and eat some breakfast. I'll be there at ten, though."

Lex arrived only ten minutes late, a new record for him. The two of them worked well together that day, and when they finished, even Elizabeth agreed they'd done a good day's work.

As they walked up the block from the Montoyas' to Jeff's house, Lex told Jeff, "I owe you an apology about Saturday. You're trying to run a business, and I did something very unprofessional."

"It takes a big man to admit he was wrong," Jeff said. "I accept your apology, Lex, but I also want you understand I won't put up with that shit again. You're twenty-two years old now, old enough to be considered a man in every conceivable way. You just have to act like one."

Jeff hoped his words would have some effect on Lex, but he doubted they would.

Five - Handling Lex With Care
May, 2002

Every spare moment Kendra and Jeff had, they spent working on the house. Jeff knew the tiny upstairs bathroom had to go. He took out all the fixtures and stored them in the basement. Then he knocked down the wall separating the bathroom from a former bedroom on the north side of the second floor. He re-framed the wall, making the bedroom smaller and the bathroom much bigger.

Jeff and Kendra picked out a heart-shaped, whirlpool tub big enough for both of them to soak in. Jeff and Lex had to cut a hole in the wall leading up the stairs to carry the massive tub up there, but Jeff didn't mind the extra drywall repair. The tub sat in the middle of an unfinished room with bare-studded walls and no ceilings. No water ran up to the second floor and neither did the drain; Jeff wasn't finished with all the plumbing repairs, and had a long way to go.

"I wish we could use the tub," Kendra said.

"No problem," a determined Jeff replied. He got the garden hose from its storage place in the basement, hooked one end of it to the showerhead on the first floor, put the other end in the bathtub and filled the tub.

Kendra took her clothes off in the drafty second floor. Once naked, she submerged herself in the warm water. As Jeff took off his clothes, Kendra looked up and said, "What's that?"

"Uh, my penis?"

"No, silly," she said, laughing. "Up there."

Jeff had torn down the ceilings to raise them to cathedral height, at Kendra's request. He followed Kendra's eyes upward. "It's a hole in the roof."

"I thought so," she said. "I was pretty sure I was looking at the sky."

Jeff got under the water with Kendra. They huddled together at the end of the tub where a faucet would be, some day. He put his arm around her. They lay back in the tub, sipped glasses of white wine and looked at the stars from their heart-shaped, whirlpool tub.

It worked well enough that Jeff and Kendra could soak away their troubles, if only until the water got cold. Later, Jeff had to siphon the dirty water out of the tub.

*****

The fixtures in the second-floor bathroom soon worked, and the kitchen functioned, but they only used these rooms when absolutely necessary. Jeff and Kendra ate all of their meals in the bedroom, which had also become the living room and the office. They felt like they lived in a one-bedroom apartment in a three thousand square foot house.

Wallpaper covered both of the first floor's living rooms and the stairway. Over the course of eighty some years it had been painted, covered over with more wallpaper, and painted again and again. The result was a thick, difficult to remove combination of wallpaper and paint. Instead of peeling off in big sheets, it came off in tiny chips.

After Jeff repaired the hole in the roof and made some drywall repairs, he decided to paint the high-ceilinged living room on the second floor.

Painting with Kendra carried its own frustrations. Since it had been his first specialty as a contractor, Jeff was a quick, efficient and accurate painter. He'd managed to teach some of his technique to Lex by the time Lex finished painting Elizabeth Montoya's windows. Jeff assumed he'd have a similar experience teaching Kendra how to paint. Far from it: by the first time he checked on her, Kendra seemed to have forgotten everything he'd showed her. He showed her again how to hold the brush, how to dip it in her work pot without picking up too much paint, how to spread the paint evenly but not too thinly.

To his amazement, when he checked on her again, Kendra was still holding the brush wrong and using too much paint. "God damn it!" Jeff yelled. "You've got that brush packed full of paint when there shouldn't be more than an inch on those bristles. You're ruining my brush. Now go rinse that off and try again. God damn it!"

"Why are you getting so upset?" Kendra asked. She sounded defensive. "I'm doing the best I can. You want me to help you, don't you?"

"No!" Jeff responded. "This isn't my house and you just help me with it, Kendra. This is your house, too, and it's as much your responsibility as it is mine. So no, I don't want you to help me. I want you to be competent at doing your own work for yourself on your own house."

"I'm not the one who's a professional remodeler," she answered. "I'm a designer for a magazine. If you want me to format the layout of this house on my laptop, that I can help you with. If you want me to be a professional painter, that's not going to happen."

"It's not going to happen with that attitude," Jeff told her. "I need you to care about this house as much as I do, Kendra."

"I do care," she insisted.

"You say you care, but your actions don't match your words. If you cared, I wouldn't have had to show you the same technique three different times; you would have gotten it right the first time if it meant that much to you. I would rather have you work on your magazine layouts than stand here with a paint brush in your hand, wasting time, if you can't even make yourself care enough about this to do it right."

Kendra seemed angry with Jeff for the rest of the day, but she paid more attention to her painting after they had this talk. She washed her brush out, shook out the excess water and started again.

Remodeling cost more than Jeff and Kendra had imagined, even with Jeff's contractor discounts. Despite having finished several projects at the Montoya's, Jeff had still, with Kendra's help, managed to use up quite a bit of the money they'd had when they bought the house. Now he had a new demand on his time: hustling up more remodeling work. He would have a hard time going out and finding work, then completing it to his customers' satisfaction, all the while getting his own house into a shape he and Kendra could live with. Not to mention he'd get married less than two months in the future. Jeff began to wonder, not for the first time, if he'd bitten off more than he and Kendra could chew.

He also worried about what to do about Lex. Lex was beginning to be more trouble than he was worth. He showed up later and later every day, and some days he didn't bother to show up at all. Jeff and Kendra both knew why: he'd been out drinking with his buddies almost every night.

Jeff told Kendra, "I don't want to be the one to have the conversation with Lex about his drinking. I like to party myself. I've even been known to do a little smoking, if I'm at the right kind of party. He's letting it rule his life, though. I used to get drunk like that when I was his age, but I was in the Navy. They weren't going to be lenient on me like I've been with Lex. I had to learn how to control myself, and so does he."

"Maybe you should tell him that," Kendra said.

"I don't want him to see me as the bad guy; he can barely stand me as it is."

She didn't bother to deny it. "Well, I'm not going to be the bad guy, either," Kendra insisted. "Lex has to be the one to decide when he's drinking too much. We're not his mother and father. He isn't going to listen to anything we tell him anyway."

"What is it about your family, Kendra? Why are you so afraid to talk to each other? I know Lex is 'sensitive,' and he breaks down and cries whenever I try to tell him anything, but someone has to put their foot down. I can't put up with his shit much longer, Kendra. Every time your brother shows up late for work, he's costing me time and money."

Kendra stormed off, claiming she had work to do.

The next morning, while she worked and Lex showed up to help Jeff with the house, he and Lex sat on the back porch and had a talk. "I've got enough work to keep you going for two weeks, Lex, but after that I don't know what's going to happen. I think you need to go find another job." Jeff knew he was firing Lex, but he wasn't about to have the family see it as that and judge him.

Lex sat there and cried. "I don't know what I'm going to do, then."

"Well, you still work part time at the restaurant."

"Yeah," Lex sniffed, "but I'm only a busser at Cloverfield's. I can't live on that salary now that I've gotten used to working for you."

They got in the van and went to work. Over the next two weeks, Jeff gave Lex some afternoons off to go job-hunting.

Six - Death's Day
December, 2011

Jonathon cradled the phone receiver between his ear and his shoulder. His wounded arm hung at his side. Blood dropped onto the carpet, and the trickle showed no signs of slowing. With his other hand he applied pressure to the bullet wound. Jeff smirked as Jonathon grimaced in pain.

Jeff was aware of the mayor's conversation with a caller Jonathon had been careful not to call by name. Jeff knew it was the police. The phone rang ten minutes after Jeff had burst into the mayor's office. Jeff had ordered the mayor to take the call.

Now, as the call ended, Jonathon took his hand off the bullet wound long enough to set the phone down on his desk. "Do you know who that was, Jeff?"

"The police," Jeff said without emotion, staring into Jonathon's eyes.

Jonathon nodded. "They say Erin's house blew up."

"Already?" Jeff said with a smile. Then he froze. He had a sinking feeling in his stomach. His smile disappeared. "No," he said. "I was inside the house. No one was home."

Jonathon shook his head. "Erin's daughter was home sick from school."

She must have triggered the explosion when she flipped on a light, or turned up the heat, Jeff thought.

The news stunned Jeff. Destroying the city planner's house had been meant to send a message, not to hurt or kill anyone. Jeff reserved that honor for Mayor Jonathon.

"Shit, shit, shit," Jeff said, stomping his foot. "I never intended to hurt an innocent person, much less a child. How was I to know the girl would be home sick? I didn't know anyone was going to be there; I specifically planned it so no one would be. I wanted Erin to know what it was like to lose her house. I didn't mean for her to lose her baby. Shit, shit, shit! I didn't want that to happen."

He hated Erin, and blamed her for his troubles every bit as much as he blamed Jonathon. They'd been partners in the sick little game they played with the town. Jeff was angry, but not heartless. Even after he'd decided to push things past the point of no return, he could still feel empathy for a mother who'd lost her daughter. There was nothing he could do about it now, though.

Jonathon took a deep breath and wiped tears from his face. "This needs to end now, Jeff. You have no idea how much danger you're in right now."

"I know exactly what I'm doing," Jeff said. "I never intended to live through this."

"There's no need to talk like that, Jeff. We can both get out of here, but we have to get out of here right now."

"Why would I want to get out of here, Jonathon? So I can go to prison? So you can keep taking away everything from me, little by little, until I'm an old man, wandering the streets, homeless? My life is over, Jonathon, and it's over because of you."

"Jeff, I..."

"Shut up! Shut the fuck up!" Jeff roared. "I told you, I am done listening to your bullshit. You try any of that smooth-talking shit again and you're dead that much quicker, you hear me?"

Outside, the firefighters made a lot of loud, banging sounds. Jeff wondered what they were doing.

While Jeff looked toward the heavy, wooden double doors, Jonathon had a moment to grab the weapon hidden under his desk. Jeff looked back, and Jonathon held a handgun aimed straight at him. Jeff didn't have time to react before he heard the piercing thunder of the weapon being fired. He felt the impact as the mayor landed the unluckiest shot in the history of firearms. The bullet had gone down the barrel of Jeff's shotgun.

Instantaneously, the shotgun exploded. Shrapnel hit the upper half of Jeff's body, tearing into his face and shoulders. The explosion forced the shell out of the barrel. It struck

Jonathon in the chest. He fell backwards, crashing into the window. He didn't attempt to catch himself as his body slumped down the wall and onto the floor.

Jeff roared with frustration. Making Jonathon suffer was the last thing he had to live for during his last few minutes on earth. The revenge he had planned was being taken away from him, all because of a one-in-a-million shot down the barrel of the shotgun.

In his fury, Jeff went to the far side of the mayor's desk. With the remains of the shotgun, Jeff beat Jonathon, holding the disabled weapon like a club. He pounded Jonathon's head into the floor, over and over, as he repeated, "Why did you do this to me? I wanted to live in peace!"

Jeff's vicious attack shattered the mayor's nose and jawbone. Blood saturated the carpet. There was no satisfaction in beating an unconscious, or already dead, man. Jeff wanted the mayor to suffer the way Jeff suffered all these years only this time, the agony would be physical instead of mental. Dead men didn't feel pain. Jeff dropped the remains of the shotgun beside Jonathon's limp body.

With his revenge thwarted, Jeff didn't know what to do while he waited for the police to come charging in through the windows or for the building to burn down around him. He paced.

Jeff's eyes fell across one of the framed prints adorning Jonathon's walls. He allowed himself to be distracted by it. It was a photo of the Civil War monument in the town's Battell Park, an obelisk surrounded by four life-sized figures in Union battle dress. The four sides of the monument were each inscribed with the names of Civil War battles in which local men had fought and lost their lives for a cause they deemed greater and more worthy than themselves.

Jeff had never paid much attention to the monument, though Battell Park meant a great deal to him. He married Kendra there almost a decade before. The heat, the sirens, and the frustration at his failure to complete his mission faded utterly from Jeff's mind as he thought back to a happier time in his life, when the house was still new to him, and the path leading to this point of no return had only begun.

Seven - Prenuptials
June, 2002

Work and the wedding consumed Jeff's time. Kendra and her mother took care of most of the wedding details. Jeff told Kendra, "You make sure the wedding is whatever you want, and tell me when to show up." He went with her when he picked out his suit, and on his own he went to two fittings in the month before the wedding.

The most pleasant wedding-related chore Kendra assigned Jeff was picking out a wedding cake. On a Saturday morning, they went to the Italian bakery near the river raceway in Willow Bend, a block from their old loft. Kendra swore they made the best cake in town. Kendra looked at the book of cake designs, and decided on a round, three-tiered cake with white butter cream frosting. The baker brought them a sample slice of each cake flavor to share. Jeff and Kendra tried white cake, chocolate, chocolate raspberry, espresso, banana, lemon, and carrot cake.

"What do you think?" Kendra asked Jeff.

"I'd be happy with any one of these, except maybe the espresso," he said. Jeff wasn't much of a coffee drinker.

"I like the banana and the carrot," Kendra said. "I think those are the two most delicious ones. Is it okay having something that different for a wedding cake, though?"

"It's your wedding," the baker said. "You serve whatever you want."

Kendra smiled. She turned to Jeff. "Banana or carrot?"

"I like them both; I want you to have what you want. Get the one you like the best."

"Then carrot it is. If anybody at the wedding doesn't like carrot cake, they don't have to eat it," Kendra said.

On the Thursday night before the wedding, Kendra and Jeff went with Candace to the reception hall. They'd both had to work, so they couldn't make it there before 8:30. One of Candace's co-workers at the court house, Barbara, catered and planned parties part-time. Barbara volunteered to decorate the hall as a favor to Candace.

Kendra chose butterflies as the wedding's theme. The guest book and the handle of the cake knife were covered in butterflies. Real butterflies gave Candace the heebie-jeebies; she didn't like to be near anything fluttering. Jeff figured Kendra was trying to send her mother a subliminal message about letting Kendra be in charge of her own weddings plans.

"No," Kendra assured him when Jeff voiced his theory. "Butterflies are the symbol of new beginnings, because they start a new life when they emerge from their cocoons."

When Barbara decorated the hall, butterflies were everywhere. Butterfly-shaped fairy lights and a dozen Mylar butterfly balloons decorated the head table.

"Are those things still going to be inflated for the reception?" Jeff asked Barbara.

"Of course," she said. "Mylar balloons last a lot longer than two days."

Jeff still had his doubts, but he did as instructed. On top of each table cloth, Kendra had Jeff tape a piece of white butcher paper to the center, as a table runner. Then she gave each table a box of crayons, so guests could doodle or write their wishes for a successful marriage and Kendra could keep them as a souvenir.

For every four chairs, one clear glass vase filled with pearlescent floral-arrangement marbles sat in the middle of the table. Barbara went around with a pitcher, filling each vase with water tinted light blue. Behind her, Candace dropped one lotus-shaped floating candle into each vase.

"Isn't this exciting?" Candace said as she helped Barbara with the centerpieces. "I mean, I know Lex will probably get married some day, but I only have one daughter. I only get to be the mother of the bride one time. Are you excited, Kendra? Or are you nervous?"

"I'm a little nervous," Kendra admitted. "Are you nervous, Jeff?"

"Should I be?" he asked. "When I talked to your dad on the phone the other night, he told me it wasn't too late to run far, far away. He told me, 'If her mother ever tells me to leave, I'm gone. '"

"He did not," Candace said.

"He did too! As a warning that I would be carrying the load, he told me about how, when Kendra and Lex were young, he used to come home from work and the grass wasn't cut, or the snow wasn't shoveled from the driveway, even though both kids had been home all day, watching TV or listening to music. He said, he used to ask them, 'What's the matter, are your arms and legs broken?' Then he'd end up mowing and shoveling himself, because if he yelled at them to do it, they'd go crying to you, Candace."

Candace laughed. Kendra sidled up to Jeff and put her arm around his waist. "We don't have to get married if you don't want to."

"Now you tell me."

"Be serious, Jeff. I mean it. We could keep living together without the marriage license. It wouldn't change much."

"I always wanted to be married," he said, kissing the top of her head. "I'm excited I'm getting to marry my best friend." He gave her a big kiss on the lips. "Even if she's a pain in my ass sometimes."

"Jeff," Barbara interrupted, "when you're finished with the table runners, will you help me bring the napkins, forks and plates in for the cake table?"

"Sure," he replied. Jeff carried everything for the wedding in from Barbara and Candace's cars. As a finishing touch, they opened the box from the chocolatier. Inside were one hundred and forty individual boxes, embossed with "Jeff and Kendra Gray, July 13, 2002" in silver letters, and two tiny wedding bells. Each box contained two mint-flavored white chocolates in the shape of butterflies, one in each of Kendra's two weddings colors, pale pink and pale green. Jeff, Kendra, and Candace set one box at each place setting while Barbara set up the cake table.

By the time they got home, after ten, Jeff and Kendra were exhausted, and starting to feel burnt out on all the planning that went into a wedding. "Two more days," Jeff thought out loud to himself. "Two more days and this will all be over."

"Then we'll officially be Mr. and Mrs. Jeff and
Kendra Gray," Kendra said.

*****

The ceremony would take place only blocks from their
home, at Battell Park. Early Friday afternoon, Jeff and Lex
swept the sidewalks and picked up trash in the park. It was a
beautiful place, up a high bank from the river. In the 1930s,
the Works Progress Administration had sponsored the building
of two sets of concrete steps up and down the bank, with an
artificial waterfall between them. Large stone planters and
islands in the middle of the human-made pond from which the
waterfall tumbled held blooming flowers. The pump that kept
the waterfall flowing was hidden in a quaint stone house that
looked like a gingerbread cottage big enough for a gnome. At
the bottom, the waterfall split into two streams that flowed into
the river. In between them grew an enormous weeping willow
tree. The waterfall and its surrounding rock garden hid behind
tall hedges.

To secure the popular park for her wedding day, Kendra
had made the reservation on the Monday after New Year's
Day. Unfortunately, the park had been at the mercy of the
public. The parks department did a good job of keeping the
lawns mowed and the trash cans emptied, but not all of the
park's patrons used the trash cans. Boxes from fast-food

chicken, chicken bones, and half-eaten corn cobs lay among the oak trees.

"You'd be proud of me," Lex said, waiting in the park when Jeff walked over to join him. "I didn't have anything to drink last night. I knew this day was too important to be late." He took a sip of coffee from an enormous cup from the convenience store down the block.

"Every day is too important to be late," Jeff told him.

Lex laughed. He took the broom and a garbage sack out of the trunk of his car, and he and Jeff swept the stairway.

"You get to meet my new roommate tonight," Lex said as they carried the first full garbage bag over to an empty trash can.

"Oh, yeah?" Jeff said. "Who is it?"

"You don't know her," Lex said.

"Her?" Jeff responded. "You're moving in with your girlfriend?"

Lex looked down at the garbage bag in his hands. "No. She and I are friends. Her name is Adrienne. She works at Cloverfield's, and I used to date her sister."

"Isn't that a little dangerous?"

"What are you talking about, Jeff?"

"I'm talking about you moving in with a woman, Lex. It's not a good idea for a man and a woman to be roommates."

"Why not?" Lex said. "Adrienne and I've been friends for more than a year now. Besides, I have a girlfriend."

"See, that's the problem. You have a girlfriend, but she's not the one who's going to be in your face every day. I've never heard of a woman and a man living together and not screwing, Lex. I don't care if you don't even think she's cute. Every girl is cute when you're drunk enough."

Lex rolled his eyes. "That's not going to happen with me and Adrienne."

That's right, Jeff thought, you're the chosen one. Things that happen to every other person in the world never happen to you.

"I'm just telling you to be careful," Jeff said. "An ounce of prevention is worth a pound of cure."

Lex ignored him, crossing to the other side of the waterfall to sweep and pick up more trash. It took them two hours to get the park clean. In the late afternoon, Kendra and the other members of the wedding party would meet them in the park. As they waited, Jeff and Lex sat on the steps of the band shell. "I want to thank you again for being my best man," Jeff told Lex.

"You don't have to thank me," Lex said. "It's an honor for me."

"It means a lot to me, you and Isaac standing up in my wedding." Isaac was Lex's best friend. They'd gone to high school together and wherever Lex was, Isaac was usually somewhere nearby. "I guess you know I haven't had much luck when it comes to friends," Jeff said. "For a long time, the closest thing I had to a best friend was my older brother Bradley."

"Kendra mentioned him," Lex said. "She said you two don't talk anymore."

Jeff couldn't hold back. The words came tumbling out. "Bradley would've made a good con artist; he found a way to talk me out of everything I had that was even remotely valuable. If he couldn't trick me out of it, he'd beat me up for it. When Bradley wasn't beating me, my mom or one of my two stepfathers was." Lex listened with a shocked expression. "That's one of the reasons I had to give up being a landlord...I couldn't put up with people taking my shit anymore. Not that I wasn't already used to having to fight for everything I owned. I was four years old when my mom took my dad away from me. Parental alienation, they call it. She made me and my brother believe he was the devil. I remember the first time Dad came around after he and Mom got divorced, when we were living with the guy who turned out to be my first stepdad. Dad brought us presents from the birthdays and Christmases he'd missed. Mom guilted me into telling Dad I didn't want his presents and giving them all back to him."

"Why would she do that to her own kid?" Lex asked. From his tone of voice, he was genuinely perplexed. Jeff knew Lex and Kendra had an easy life.

Jeff shrugged. "I don't know; maybe she was a sociopath. My brother was a sociopath. We stopped physically fighting when I got into my twenties, but the mental abuse never stopped. I got tired of him taking advantage of me, using guilt to talk me into working for him for free and not even showing the least bit of gratitude for how I bent over backwards to please him. Finally, I decided I didn't need him in my life anymore. I deserve to have people treat me with respect. If they won't treat me with respect, they can go to hell. I had to get them out of my life. I don't trust people easily, Lex."

"I'm sorry," Lex said quietly.

Jeff wasn't finished, though. "The last male friend I had," he continued, "broke into my home and attacked me in the middle of the night. He thought I was sleeping with his girlfriend, which I wasn't. I thought he was going to kill me. It made it that much harder to trust people, now that I have to be concerned about my safety, and my life, all the time."

"What did you do?" Lex asked.

"I jabbed his eye out with my thumb and told him to get out. The next day I moved. I had to drive around in circles for two weeks so I could finish taking care of my customers without him finding me. That's what brought me back home to Princess City."

Jeff let the silence hang in the air for a moment. Then he and Lex changed the subject, talking about movies until Kendra and the others arrived.

Two of Kendra's friends from college, Marie Sipski and Ellis Cho, were to be Kendra's bridesmaids. Wade, Candace, Isaac, Marie and Ellis joined them in the park late that afternoon. It seemed funny to be preparing for a wedding when everyone was wearing shorts and t-shirts.

As Kendra's family and their friends stood, looking around the park, engaging in idle chit-chat and waiting for someone to tell them what to do, Jeff assumed the leader role by default. He decided where he and Kendra should stand, how the groomsmen and bridesmaids would line up on either side of them, where the folding chairs should start and stop, and when Candace would start the CD player. The rehearsal took them about an hour. Then everyone went home to get cleaned up for the rehearsal dinner.

The running joke in the Wilson family went: after the Wilsons spent so much on Kendra's college education, they would celebrate her wedding rehearsal dinner at Taco Bell.

For a while, they'd considered it. In the end, though, Kendra decided she wanted a nice dinner at a steak restaurant. Since according to tradition the groom's parents took care of the rehearsal dinner, but Jeff didn't have any contact with his parents, Jeff and Kendra saved up some money to pay for it.

When Jeff and Kendra arrived at the restaurant, the host took them back to their table. Lex, Isaac and Adrienne (Jeff presumed) were already there. Lex and Isaac each had a draft beer. Adrienne, who looked like she was still under twenty-one, had an icy soda instead.

Jeff recognized Adrienne as one of the hostesses at Cloverfield's. She was a beautiful girl, but she didn't seem to know it. Though tall, she seemed embarrassed about her height. She slouched. Her blunt haircut didn't flatter her heart-shaped face. Her thick makeup, punctuated by green eye shadow, didn't match her light blue dress, or her blue eyes.

"Jeff, Kendra, this is Adrienne Newton," Lex said as they took their seats. Kendra sat at the head of the table, and Jeff sat to her right, across from Lex.

"So you're the new roommate!" Jeff said.

"Yeah," Adrienne said. "I'm so excited. We're getting our apartment next week."

Kendra glared at Jeff. "What?"

"We're moving in together," Lex said.

"I didn't even know you two were dating," Kendra said when she'd recovered from a coughing fit. She'd almost choked on her ice water. Jeff patted her back gently.

"We're not," Lex explained. "We're just friends. We are going to be roommates, though."

"Oh," Kendra said. "Congratulations."

"Congratulations to you, too," Adrienne said back. "Do you guys think we should order an appetizer, or should we wait until everyone else gets here?"

As she said this, Candace and Wade arrived. Wade sat beside Jeff, with Candace on the other side of him. "I've never eaten here before," Candace said as she hung her purse on the back of her chair and sat down.

"I have," Wade said. "Order the prime rib and you'll be fine."

"What if I want lobster?"

"Then order lobster," Kendra told her.

The last two members of their party, Ellis and Marie, along with Ellis's boyfriend Sun, joined them shortly after Wade and Candace arrived, taking the last three seats at the far end of the table. Wade took the initiative in ordering appetizers.

At her turn to order a drink, Kendra asked the server, "What goes good with red meat?"

"How about a glass of the house burgundy?" he suggested.

"Sounds good," she said. "I'm going to eat steak like you've never seen me eat steak before," she warned the table.

Jeff ordered a Guinness and told the server to keep them coming.

As they looked over their menus, Ellis said across the table to Kendra, "Did I tell you Sun and I had to get rid of Princess?"

"No way," Kendra said. "But you loved that crazy little mutt. Why?"

"I have allergies," Sun told them. He looked around the table and paused for a second before adding, "What, no one's going to make the joke about the Korean couple eating their dog?"

Lex and Isaac's laughter sounded nervous. Wade responded, "I ate some dog while I was in Korea. This was ten, fifteen years ago, while I was in the Air Force reserves. You know, it wasn't half bad."

"You buy dog, make good soup," Jeff joked. Everyone laughed.

Kendra said, "I'm not sure how to follow that up. Let's change the subject. I think I'll have the prime rib. Anybody else know what they want to order?"

Most of them ordered prime rib. As she waited for everyone to finish eating, Kendra looked at Lex and whispered, "Do Mom and Dad know you and Adrienne are moving in together?"

Lex smirked. "Of course," he said. "There's nothing to hide, because we're just going to be roommates…unlike you and Jeff. They don't have a problem with it."

"Touché," she said.

As they got up to leave, Candace came over to Jeff and Kendra's end of the table. "You know, Kendra, you could spend the night at our house. That way, Jeff won't see you before the wedding."

"Candace, I've seen Kendra every day for the past two and half years, and I'm going to see her every day for the rest of my life," Jeff said. "I'm not superstitious about things like that. I want to see Kendra's face when I wake up tomorrow morning, to remind me why I want to get married in the first place."

"You're sweet," Kendra said. She turned around and kissed him full on the mouth.

"Okay, we'd better go," Candace said. Kendra waved goodbye to her without taking her lips from Jeff's mouth.

On the way home, Kendra asked Jeff, "Do you think we'll be able to sleep tonight? Or will we be too excited?"

"I'll be able to sleep," he said.

Jeff wasn't a worrier like Kendra and her mother, but he was a problem-solver. He sometimes woke up early in the morning to think a problem over until he came up with a solution. The wedding wasn't a problem, of course, but Jeff knew when the sun rose the next morning, he'd be lying in bed thinking about what he had to do.

Eight - Best Day of Their Lives
July, 2002

The morning of Jeff and Kendra's wedding was bright and hot. Kendra left early with her mother to have their hair, makeup and nails done, but only after Jeff woke her up early to make sure they got in one more session of single-people sex.

Jeff threw on a pair of shorts and got in his van. Figuring he'd need the van to take the wedding gifts home, he dropped the vehicle off at the reception hall. The kitchen crew was already there, getting ready. They let Jeff in, and he made a few changes he hadn't wanted to make in front of Candace and Barbara. He straightened the string of lights behind the head table and moved some of the decorations. Then he called a taxi from his cell phone and got a ride to Battell Park.

Since Kendra had declared herself too nervous to eat breakfast, Jeff hadn't had anything to eat either. He went to a diner near the park. He and Kendra had eaten there once before. His appetite was good, despite the fact he was nervous, too. He ate a hearty breakfast of round steak and eggs. Jeff said to the waitress, "I'm getting married today!"

"That's exciting," she said back. "Your first marriage?"

"First and only," he said. On his way out, he stopped by every other patron's table and told them, "I'm getting married today!"

Most of them nodded their heads and said, "That's great." One of the older men said, "Why would you want to do that to yourself?" Jeff only smiled and kept walking; he heard a chuckle behind him.

On his walk back toward the house, Jeff had a terrible case of heartburn. By the time he'd walked home, Lex and Isaac were waiting for him on the front porch.

"This is a cool house," Isaac remarked, looking around at the exterior. "I like your front door."

"Thanks," Jeff said. "Kendra picked that out, It was one of the first things we did to the house." He let them in. Once inside, Jeff got the antacids from the medicine cabinet in the bathroom and took a generous handful.

The three of them each picked a room to get dressed in. Jeff paired his charcoal gray suit with a white shirt and an off-white tie. The groomsmen wore the same suit, but in a lighter shade of gray, with white shirts and gray ties. Kendra had personally approved all of the colors, which she declared proper for a late-morning, outdoor, summer wedding.

The men sat on the couch to watch TV. They were joined by Wade Wilson after a little while. He wore a dark gray suit with a dark gray shirt. Jeff called it his "gangster suit."

As they waited, the florist van pulled up, and Jeff helped the delivery woman bring in the flowers. Then he had to separate them: the boutonnieres for himself, the two groomsmen, and Wade; corsages for the bridesmaids and Candace; a floral centerpiece for the top tier of the wedding cake; and the bride's bouquet. Jeff got out a roll of masking tape and a black permanent marker and labeled the various flowers so he wouldn't mix them up. His boutonniere had a pink carnation; the groomsmen and father of the bride had white carnations.

After about an hour, Kendra and her mother showed up, along with Ellis and Marie. Candace told Jeff to go to the back of the house, where he wouldn't see Kendra as she went up to the bedroom to get dressed.

Jeff and Kendra's ceremony would take place inside the band shell, officiated by a justice of the peace. They'd rented a hundred folding chairs for their guests, which the rental company set up for them. They'd also set up a card table, covered in an elegant white lace tablecloth, with one box containing the couple's wedding programs and another for receiving wedding cards.

A pale green basket with a butterfly ribbon on the handle held about a hundred store-bought, polished river stones. A printed card next to the basket instructed wedding guests to take one stone, to be used following the ceremony, though it didn't explain why.

Jeff, Lex and Isaac arrived at the park in Lex's car, still littered with discarded fast-food wrappers and empty cigarette packs. The car reeked of cigarette smoke; Jeff hoped he wouldn't smell like cigarettes by the time they reached the park, six blocks away. Kendra stayed behind with her parents.

When he arrived at the park, Jeff introduced himself to the judge who would marry him. She was a young woman in a business-like light purple dress. He thought she said her name was Judge Renfrew, but he didn't quite catch it. He knew she was Candace's favorite judge at the court house, and it had been easy for Candace to convince her to marry Candace's daughter.

As he and the judge stood, waiting for Kendra, Jeff noticed someone had tripped over the white runner on the grass, separating the two columns of folding chairs. Jeff stepped off the band shell and smoothed it back into place. A few moments later, though, one of Kendra's cousins tripped over the thing while trying to make her way to her seat. Jeff hopped down again and tugged the runner back into place.

This time, when he got back up on the band shell, Jeff addressed the growing crowd of wedding guests. "Would everybody please watch their step on the runner?"

Marie and Ellis were the next to arrive at the park, in Marie's car. No two women ever had more opposite body types than Marie Sipski and Ellis Cho. Marie, tall and thin as a rail, had no visible curves. Even her hips were straight vertical planes. She'd curled her blonde hair into ringlets. Ellis, short and stocky, had rounded shoulders and an apple shape. She'd decorated her shiny, straight blue-black hair with daisy barrettes.

Kendra had found it impossible to choose one dress that looked equally good on Marie and Ellis, so instead she chose a color (rum pink, the boutique called it) and let them each pick out their own dresses. Marie chose a low-backed, spaghetti-strap sheath dress. Ellis chose a short-sleeved, high-waisted gown with a big sash in the front that covered her midsection. Only their handbags matched: tiny white satin things with handles of crystal beads. Kendra would carry this same handbag with crystal beads sewn onto the front in the shape of a butterfly.

Jeff waited on the band shell for forty-five minutes. Eleven o'clock came and went. Wade's car finally pulled up, but for a moment, no one stepped out. Just when Jeff wondered if Kendra had changed her mind, Wade got out and opened the back door for Kendra. She got out of the car. She turned to face the band shell, blinking in the bright sunlight. She saw Jeff and smiled, glowing. He couldn't remember if he'd ever seen her looking happier.

Jeff had seen Kendra's dress on the hanger, but never on Kendra. The bodice of her cap-sleeved, modestly cut dress was cream-colored and embroidered with rum-pink flowers with mint-green stems. The colors were subtle, like the mint green of the dress's tulle skirt. Kendra looked perfect.

Jeff couldn't take his eyes off her. She and her father talked and laughed. The judge stepped to the front of the band shell and said, "Are we ready to begin the ceremony?" Jeff nodded. "Then let's begin."

Candace started the CD player, and Kendra's father walked her up the aisle to the sounds of Bach's "Air on the G String."

As Wade walked Kendra toward the band shell, Jeff felt nervous. He was glad he and Kendra were reading their vows and that he didn't have to memorize them, because his mind went blank. Although they'd rehearsed all these details the night before, he stood in the wrong spot, and the judge had to prompt him. Kendra climbed the stairs, wiping a tear from her eye as Wade let go of her hand. Wade went to his seat in the front row. As Kendra joined Jeff on the band shell, Jeff knew this was exactly where he wanted to be.

The judge talked about what a nice day it was for a wedding and how lucky the couple was to have their family and friends here with them. She read a passage from a book about the wedding being the public symbol of the couple's private decision to spend the rest of their lives together.

Lex handed Jeff his vows. Jeff read the vows, which he had written himself, in a clear, loud voice. Kendra read hers, but her voice was so soft, Jeff knew he was the only one who could hear her. It didn't matter: the words were intended for no one but him.

Lex gave Kendra and Jeff their rings; Jeff put the ring on Kendra's finger first. When she put the ring on his finger, he pulled her in for a kiss, and the band shell faded away. Nothing existed in this universe but the two of them, connected, forever. The judge pronounced them husband and wife. They signed their marriage certificate; Lex and Ellis signed as witnesses. Their friends and family applauded as they kissed again.

After the photographer had taken a few staged photos on the band shell, Jeff once again addressed the wedding guests. "We asked you all to take a river stone before the ceremony," he explained. "These are wishing stones. Kendra and I are going to lead a procession down one side of the steps to the river. We'll toss our stones in the water and make a wish. We hope you'll follow us and make a wish with us, as long as you don't have a problem with climbing stairs. We'll come back up the other side, and then proceed with the receiving line."

Jeff and Kendra crossed the lawn, walking down the stairs by the waterfall to the edge of the river. When they reached the weeping willow, they saw a man in bicycle shorts, sitting with his back propped against the stone wall, staring out at the river.

"You've got to get out of here," Jeff told the man.

"What, do you own the park or something?" the man asked.

"I do today," Jeff said.

The man hesitated and seemed to think over his options for a moment. He looked at Jeff and Kendra and the long line of people following them. Then he picked up his bike and carried it up the stairs, riding out of sight when he reached the top.

Jeff and Kendra threw their stones and made their wishes. Each of their guests threw a stone into the river with good-luck wishes for the newlywed couple.

Afterward, Jeff and Kendra stood on the grass in front of the hedge row and formed a receiving line. Jeff got so wrapped up in the wedding ceremony and Kendra, he hadn't taken much time to look around at who had attended the ceremony.

Jeff and Kendra shook their guests' hands and accepted congratulations from Kendra's Uncle Alex and her Aunt

Florence. Alex was Candace's brother, and Lex's namesake. Wade and Candace each had one brother and one sister, and all those aunts and uncles were married with children. Kendra had a host of cousins. Jeff had only one cousin he had any type of contact with. His cousin Sarah, her husband Rob, and their two daughters were the only members of Jeff's family present. Inviting anyone else would've stirred up too many painful memories and caused too many problems.

It took almost a half hour for Jeff and Kendra to greet all of their wedding guests. When the receiving line was done, Jeff and Kendra had to pose for photos in the rock garden, along with the maids of honor and the groomsmen.

By the time the photographer finished, they were hot and thirsty. They had another hour before the reception, so they stopped into Cloverfield's. Lex, Isaac, Marie and Ellis came along.

The men each ordered a Guinness. Kendra had a lemon drop martini, and Marie had an appletini. Ellis didn't usually drink. "Do you know how to make a Golden Cadillac?" she asked the bartender.

"I've never heard of it," the bartender said. "Do you know what's in it?"

"I know it's an ice cream drink," she said. "I think it has Galliano. Hey, guys, does anybody know what's in a Golden Cadillac?"

"Yeah," Jeff joked. "A billionaire." Everyone laughed.

No one knew the actual ingredients, so Ellis ordered a simple vanilla milkshake.

Being in Cloverfield's gave them all a chance to relax in an air-conditioned dining room and be themselves, despite their formal clothes. Jeff and Kendra had met at the bar in Cloverfield's while Kendra worked part-time as a hostess. It felt like a second home to them.

When Jeff finished his beer, Lex bought him another. Then it was time to go to the reception hall. The bridal party made their formal entrance to Classical and easy-listening dinner music. A DJ interrupted the music to say, "I present to you Mr. and Mrs. Gray." The guests applauded. Jeff choked up with pride as they went to the head table.

"Can you run to the bar and get me a beer?" Jeff asked Lex. Lex nodded, and asked Kendra if she wanted anything. She said no. Lex left, and came back from the bar a few minutes later with his hands loaded with three beers: one for Jeff, one for himself, and one for Isaac. While dinner was served, the open bar closed.

The kitchen crew made a traditional Polish-American wedding dinner: fried chicken, Polish sausage, mashed potatoes and gravy, buttered noodles, sweet cabbage, bread rolls, green beans, and pies. Some of the pies were apple, some were lemon custard, and some were chocolate pudding. The crew served the meal family-style, with dishes being passed from person to person. Jeff loved this food, and he ate two plates full. He noticed Kendra didn't eat much, though he'd helped her load her plate.

"Eat something," he told her. "If you drink that champagne on an empty stomach, it will go straight to your head."

"I'm trying," she said, picking at a chicken drumstick with her fork. "My stomach doesn't feel very good. I'm nervous."

"Why are you nervous now? The hard part is over."

She looked at him. "The planning was the hard part. Now that we're officially married, I couldn't be happier. I feel like I'm putting on a performance, though. Do you know what I mean? I almost feel like we're in a play."

"It's still a party," he said. "Enjoy it as much as you can." She kissed him and everyone let out an "Aww!"

Kendra managed to finish her drumstick and some of her mashed potatoes. She needed her strength, since soon after dinner, Jeff and Kendra had their first dance. The opening notes of U2's "All I Want Is You" began, and Kendra put her arms around Jeff.

"I wish we'd taken ballroom dancing lessons," she whispered to him.

"Relax," he said. "You're a good dancer. Follow my lead."

She relaxed, and they moved around the dance floor with effortless grace. Jeff raised her arm over her head and spun Kendra around flaring out the bottom of her dress. Jeff didn't care about the song. All he cared about was right there in his arms, moving when he moved, with her arms around him.

When their first dance ended, Kendra and Wade danced to "Because You Loved Me." Jeff sat back down and watched from the head table, smiling at the way Wade and Kendra cracked jokes to keep each other laughing so neither one would start crying. They were successful until the second chorus, when Kendra couldn't hold back her happy-sad tears any longer. Of course, when she cried, Wade cried too.

After the father-daughter dance, the DJ started the party music. The guests enjoyed themselves for five songs or so before the DJ announced it was time for the bouquet and garter tosses. The crowd on the dance floor made a circle, with Kendra in the middle, and all the single women lined up behind her. Marie, Ellis and Adrienne were in the front.

Kendra's bouquet was actually three smaller bouquets, tied individually with plain white ribbon, and then tied together with a wide, pink ribbon. She took the pink ribbon off in the middle of the dance floor, then tossed the three sections of bouquet behind her head. Jeff's cousin Sarah's younger daughter, age four, caught the first section. Adrienne caught the second. Ellis caught the third; she promptly brought it to Sun's table and waved it in his face. "See? You have to marry me now," she told him.

Then the DJ brought a folding chair to the middle of the floor and had Kendra sit in it. She pulled up the tulle of her dress high enough to expose the garter on her thigh: white, with a mint-green ribbon and a little gold butterfly charm. Jeff knelt in front of her, kissed the inside of her thigh, and took her garter off with his teeth, as the guests once again burst into sounds of whoops and applause for the couple. Jeff snickered as he used his hands to take the garter off from around Kendra's sandal. He tossed it into the ring of unattached men all around him. The crowd went wild when Isaac caught it. Moments later, Candace went around and collected the garter and reunited the three sections of flowers.

The last formality of the evening was the cutting of the cake. As they neared the cake table, prompted by the photographer and her assistant, Kendra repeated the warning she'd given Jeff the night before: "If you smash the cake into my face, even a little bit, there isn't going to be any honeymoon."

"Got it," he assured her. He had no intention of doing anything to make her unhappy. When the photographer set up,

Kendra took the butterfly-handled cake knife and cut a small piece. She and Jeff each took a fork, and they carefully fed one another a tiny morsel. It was picture-perfect.

Kendra cut them each a full piece of cake, then passed the cake-cutting responsibilities off to Barbara and to her Aunt Florence. Wade went around and passed out cigars. He was a cigar aficionado and had brought two boxes of fine ones. Jeff took two, lighting up one of them with Wade.

"I think the play is over now," he told Kendra. "Now we can really relax and have fun."

For the next five hours, they talked with friends, danced, smoked cigars, and drank. They found wedding guests kept bringing them drinks from the bar. Kendra drank far more than Jeff had ever seen her drink before; he was amazed she could still stand on her feet. Toward the end of the night, Jeff switched to lemon-lime soda since he knew he would be driving himself and Kendra to their honeymoon destination. When most of the guests started leaving, Candace and Barbara began the clean-up, and Jeff and Kendra stayed to help. Lex helped them put their wedding gifts in the back of their van.

"You two should go now," Candace told them. "We'll finish cleaning up here; you go enjoy your honeymoon."

Kendra kissed her mother's cheek. "Thanks, Mom, for everything." Kendra thanked her father, then went around saying good night to the guests who remained.

As she did, Jeff took Wade aside. "I think Lex's had too much to drink," he told his father-in-law. "Someone needs to take his keys away from him and give him a ride home. I can call him a taxi if you want."

"That's okay," Wade said. "His mom and I'll take him home. He can sober up at our place for a little while, and then I'll drive him back here to get his car."

"That'll work," Jeff agreed. "I'd hate to have everybody remember our wedding as the day Lex got a DUI."

Wade shook his head. "I'll take care of it; thanks for saying something." The two men hugged before Jeff and Kendra said their final goodbyes and got into the van.

"That was a hell of a party," Jeff said as they drove off. "I can't remember when I've had more fun."

"It was fun," Kendra agreed. "Now I'm tired."

"Me, too." Jeff was glad they already had reservations at a hotel room for the night. They entered the room, and Kendra went straight to the bed and took the bobby pins out of her hair. Jeff ran water in the hot tub. "Do you want to get naked?" he asked her.

"Not yet," she said. "I'm pretty hungry."

"I'm starving," Jeff said. "Want to order room service?"

Kendra called room service and ordered mushroom ravioli and a mushroom-Swiss burger. As they waited, Kendra turned on the TV. The premium cable station was showing Monsters Inc.

"I've been wanting to see this," Kendra said. "It looks cute."

Jeff didn't argue. The food arrived, and Jeff and Kendra ate in the tub, watching the cartoon. When they finished, Jeff got out of the tub and cleared away the takeout containers.

"Let me remind you, I didn't smash any cake in your face today."

Kendra got out of the tub, dried off and pushed Jeff down on the bed. "It's time for your reward," she said. They made love and fell asleep.

Jeff and Kendra spent Sunday morning in the hotel room. They slept late and had a late brunch. That afternoon, they packed and took off to Kentucky, where they would spend their honeymoon visiting Mammoth Cave.

Nine - It Begins
July, 2002

After helping Jeff carry the luggage into the house, Kendra checked the mail. Jeff saw her holding an envelope when he came out of the bathroom. "What's that?" he asked.

"It's a letter from code enforcement," she told him. "It says there's construction debris in our yard, and if we don't have it cleaned up within the next two weeks, they can give us a fine of up to two hundred dollars."

"Well, there is a pile of busted-up concrete back there," Jeff said. "I guess people can see it from the florist's parking lot, even if they can't really see it from the road. I'll throw it in the trash trailer and take it to the dump some time this week. Don't worry about it."

Jeff had many code enforcement letters when he was a landlord in Willow Bend. He knew as long as he complied, he would be left alone.

He didn't think much about it. On Monday he went to work as usual. On Tuesday morning when Kendra was already at work, Jeff noticed the letter from the city sitting on the ladder in the front room. He went outside to load the concrete onto the trash trailer. The trash sat there for a few more days, before he started a new drywall job and had a load of old drywall to throw away. Then he got rid of it, before the ten-day deadline. Jeff forgot about it and went back to work.

One morning as Jeff walked through the dining room, he saw a woman in the front yard. A brown SUV sat parked, blocking the florist's parking lot. Jeff opened the front door and said to her, "Is there something I can help you with?"

The woman, in her late forties with long, dark hair, shook her head. "No, sir," she said. "I'm just doing my job for code enforcement."

"What are you doing in my yard?" he asked from the front door.

"I'm looking around," she said. "There's been a complaint about you having trash in your yard."

"I got a letter about that a few weeks ago," Jeff said. He stepped out onto the porch and closed the door behind him. "There was some construction debris in the back yard, and I took it to the garbage dump. I'm a contractor, so sometimes I have construction materials in my yard. I always take care of it, though."

"I'm aware of the previous complaint," she said. "There's been another complaint."

"From who?" Jeff asked.

"I can't tell you that," she insisted. "Complaints are confidential."

"I want to know who thinks it's any of their business what I do in my own yard," Jeff said. "This is my property."

She looked sour. "Sir," she said, "I'm here on behalf of the town, doing my job. Would you please go back in your house?"

Jeff was pissed off. He didn't like anyone talking to him like they were his boss on his own property. "Why don't you get the fuck off my property and do your work from the sidewalk? And move your God-damned truck. You're blocking the florist parking lot!"

"Don't tell me what to do, sir," she said, taking a step toward him, her finger pointed toward his face.

"Go away, lady," Jeff said, sick and tired of this conversation. The code enforcement officer turned and walked to her car. As she walked away, Jeff uttered, "Bitch."

Jeff went to work, but when he came home for the afternoon, he called town hall. "I want to talk to the mayor," he said.

"Mr. Thompson isn't in his office right now," the woman who answered the phone said. "If you tell me what your call is regarding, I may be able to help you."

"Who am I speaking to?"

"My name is Rachelle Bowen; I'm the mayor's secretary."

"Well, Rachelle, I had one of your code enforcement officers in my yard today, and I'm not very happy about it. That lady acted like she owned the place and I was some trespasser. I know she has to do her job, but she's a public servant. She works for me. She doesn't have to give me a damn attitude while she's on my property. She was a short lady with brown hair, not really young. Do you know the one I'm talking about?"

Rachelle laughed. "Her name is Katherine Tate. She's been working for code enforcement for fifteen years now."

"The way you laughed makes me think you agree with me," Jeff said. "It sounds like you've had other calls about her."

"Let me transfer your phone call to Earl McGhee's office. Earl is the head of code enforcement. He's out with the mayor right now, but you could leave your complaint in Earl's voice mail."

"Thank you," Jeff said. "That would be fine."

Rachelle transferred the call, and Jeff left his message.

When Earl returned Jeff's call, he apologized. "I'm sorry Kate talked to you the way she did, Mr. Gray. I spoke to her about it. I only hope you understand she has to be able to do her job."

"I don't have a problem with your officers doing their job. I have a problem with them walking around my yard like they own it. I have a problem with your officer getting up in my face and shaking her finger. When somebody gets in my face like that, I take it as a challenge."

"I'm sure she wasn't trying to threaten you, Mr. Gray. I've known Kate for years, and I've never seen her threaten a citizen."

"But you weren't in my yard that day, and you're not sure about anything. All you have is my word and hers, and I bet her side of the story is completely different from mine."

"Her side of the story is a little different, but I assumed you were telling me the truth, and I had a talk with her."

"The next time someone makes a complaint about my house, could you send someone else to investigate it? Could you investigate it yourself?"

Earl laughed. He had a deep voice, and Jeff didn't even have to see him to imagine what he looked like: a tall, heavyset man with a large frame, probably in his sixties if not older. "I can't guarantee that, Mr. Gray. If Kate is the officer I have in your area, she's the one I'm going to send to your house."

"My area is your area," Jeff insisted. "I'm right across the river from town hall. I can see your roof from the second floor of my house." The town hall was on Cedar Street, one block south of the main thoroughfare, Lincoln Way. "All of your officers are in my area when they're sitting in their offices."

"I see where you're coming from, Mr. Gray," Earl said. "I'll do what I can about making sure my officers are respectful to you and your property, but that's all I can promise you."

Jeff got off the phone, still unhappy. Over the next few months, he and Kendra received two more letters from code enforcement about various issues with the exterior of the house. They took care of the minor issues right away, and didn't have to deal face-to-face with the code enforcement officers. Now it was clear they were trying to show him who was boss.

In August 2003, Jeff and Kendra sat on their couch watching television when the phone rang. Kendra, closer to the phone, picked it up. "Hello?" After a short conversation, she hung up and said, "That was Lex."

"What did he want?"

"He wouldn't tell me. He says he'd rather talk about it in person. We're supposed to meet him at Western Atlantic at four tomorrow. I wonder what it's about."

"Me too," Jeff said. "He's probably going to tell us he's gay." Jeff had long held the theory that Lex was secretly gay.

"Probably," Kendra agreed. "He could have told us years ago. It's not like we're going to have a problem with it."

Jeff wondered, but Lex and his problems weren't the top priority in his mind. He had a full work schedule, and as always, there were a thousand things to be done to the house. He didn't think much about it until the next day, when Kendra reminded him they had an appointment with Lex.

When Jeff and Kendra walked in to the fine dining restaurant, Lex sat at the near end of the bar, nursing a beer. At this time of the afternoon, the restaurant was closed. The bar was open, but no one was there except Lex.

"Hey," Kendra said to Lex as she sat down next to him. Jeff sat on the other side of Kendra.

"Let me get you something to drink," Lex said, getting up from his bar stool. He went around to the other side of the bar and, without even asking, poured Jeff a tall draft Guinness. "What are you having?" he asked Kendra.

"Just a Diet Coke, with no ice," she said. Lex poured her soda, then sat back down in front of his beer. He took a long sip.

"So, what do you want to talk about?" Kendra asked her brother. Jeff cracked a grin.

Lex let out a sigh, then got right to the point. "Adrienne is pregnant."

Jeff was taking a gulp of beer at that moment and had a hard time swallowing it. Once he got the beer down he and Kendra stared. Kendra broke the silence by saying, "You got Adrienne pregnant?"

Lex shrugged and took another long sip of his beer. "She says I'm the father, but I know she was sleeping with two other guys. It only happened one time. We were watching this porno movie, and things just…happened."

Jeff couldn't imagine people watching porn together without the outcome of something sexual "just happening."

"Watching porn together? Just the two of you?" Jeff said.

"We were drunk." Lex muttered. Not answering Jeff's question.

Jeff didn't have to read Lex's mind to know who the two other guys were that were getting Adrienne. He wouldn't put having a four-way past those two, especially given the character of some of Lex's friends, and the steady flow of alcohol taking place inside the apartment.

"What are you going to do?" Kendra asked him. "What's Adrienne going to do? Did she just find out, or has she known about this for a while?"

Her line of questioning probably would have continued, but Lex cut her off. "She took the pregnancy test at home last week, and she went to the doctor and confirmed it yesterday. She says she's keeping the baby. I was drunk. I didn't even know what I was doing. Adrienne wasn't drinking, though. She's not even going to be twenty-one until October."

"Like that would stop her." Jeff interjected.

Lex continued, "She'll miss out on going to the bars for her birthday because she'll be pregnant. The doctor told her the due date is going to be some time in February."

"Wow," Kendra said. "I can't believe it."

"I can believe it," Jeff said. "You say you were drunk did you give her permission to have sex with you? Were you a willing participant?"

"No," Lex said. "I was really drunk. I didn't know what was going on."

"Well, that's rape," Jeff said. "She raped your ass."

"No, no, I wasn't raped," Lex said.

Jeff continued, "I told you it wasn't a good idea when you and Adrienne moved in together. I told you this was going to be trouble. That is how you feel about it, isn't it? Or should I be saying 'Congratulations?'"

Lex tapped his empty beer mug against the counter before getting up and pouring himself another. As he poured, he said, "You should be saying 'Congratulations,' and you should be kicking my ass for being such a fucking idiot."

"Well, you're damned either way," Jeff said. "If you ignore Adrienne during her pregnancy, and the baby turns out to be yours, you'll feel bad about missing out. On the other hand, if you assume it is yours, and it turns out to be someone else's, you'll be emotionally invested in someone you can't keep. Not to mention what it'll do to your mother...you have to pick one extreme or the other; that's my advice."

Lex nodded, but Kendra was stuck on something Lex had mentioned earlier. "You mean you didn't use protection?" she asked, although from the look on her face, she really didn't want to picture her brother's sex life.

"I was drunk," he said.

"That's no excuse," Kendra muttered. "You need to protect yourself from diseases. You should know that, since your last girlfriend gave you that cold sore, and you're lucky it was just oral herpes and not the other kind."

Jeff shook his head and got up to pour himself another beer. Jeff had sucked the first one down too fast to wait around on Lex's invitation.

"I know, I know," Lex said as he sat back down. "I'm not saying it wasn't stupid. I'm not saying I have anyone to blame but myself."

"Speaking of girlfriends," Kendra chimed in, "does Nicole know about this?"

"She doesn't know, and she doesn't need to know," Lex said. "She and I broke up a couple weeks ago."

"She probably didn't like the idea of you living with another woman," Kendra said.

"She probably didn't like you watching porn with another woman…and her friends," Jeff added. "I don't care what a girl looks like; if you're going to watch porn with her, you're going to end up fucking her."

"We only watch it because it's funny," Lex said with a smirk. "The dialogue and the acting are so horrible, they're always more funny than sexy."

"Yet Adrienne ended up pregnant," Kendra said, almost under her breath, as she took another sip of her Coke. "This whole situation is far from ideal, Lex."

"I know, I know," he said again.

"Have you told Mom and Dad?"

"Yeah," he said. "I sat them down and had a talk with them last night. Dad didn't say much of anything. Mom was angry, but she was also excited."

"Of course she was excited," Jeff said. "She's going to be a grandparent for the first time; your mom would be excited about that." He took another sip of his beer, grinning his "I told you so" grin.

Kendra said, "She's always been disappointed you and I decided not to have kids." She thought for a moment, then added, "At least this will take some of the pressure off our backs."

"Good luck, man," Jeff said. "If there's anything we can do to help, let us know. Kendra and I can baby-sit. Believe it or not, I used to be a great babysitter when I was a teenager. Kids like me. All my mom's friends used to let me watch their kids, and I had fun doing it."

"I'm going to be an aunt," Kendra said, sounding awed. "We're going to be Aunt Kendra and Uncle Jeff."

"Yeah," Jeff said, "and Lex is going to be a 'Daddy'. Too bad it wasn't a job he volunteered for."

"Are you and Adrienne dating now?" Kendra asked. "I know this is sudden, but have you started making plans to get married?"

Lex finished off his second beer and shuddered. "No. No way in hell. Not a chance: zip, zero, nada. I don't feel that way about Adrienne. I like her, she and I are friends, but there's nothing remotely romantic going on between us. I can't imagine there will ever be a day when there will be. I'll never marry her."

"You say that now," Jeff said, "but everything's going to change once she has your baby. She's a friend you got drunk and screwed now, but in February she's going to be the mother of your child. Your feelings will change; you wait and see." Jeff's mug was empty again, so Lex got up and poured him a third Guinness.

"You've never been in this situation," Lex said. "You don't know that."

"I have a pretty good record of predicting what's going to happen, though," Jeff countered. "I told you not to move in with Adrienne in the first place."

"This may turn out to be the best thing that's ever happened to you," Kendra said philosophically, laying her hand on Lex's shoulder. "You might enjoy the responsibility of caring for a child."

"I might, but I might also not enjoy the expense of raising a child."

"Learn from your mistakes, though," Jeff advised him. "Don't ever let this happen again, with Adrienne or with any other girl, unless you and that woman make the conscious decision to get pregnant. It's not fair to your future son or daughter to bring them into this world haphazardly."

"He's right," Kendra said. "That said, we're both behind you. Anything you need, you call us."

"Do yourself and your mother a favor, though, and have a DNA test," Jeff added. He finished off his beer, and Kendra gave her brother a hug. Jeff hugged him too. "This might be a lot of worry about nothing. You might take a DNA test and find out this is some other poor sucker's problem."

"In some ways I hope I do, and in other ways I hope I don't," Lex said. "I always knew I wanted to have children. Hell, when Nicole and I first got together, we were talking about having a big family, seven or eight kids."

"Nicole was raised Catholic," Kendra explained to Jeff.

"I've always been excited about fatherhood…I just wasn't expecting it to happen this soon, or with Adrienne."

Jeff took out his credit card to pay for the beers and the Diet Coke, but Lex brushed him off. "It's on me," Lex said.

As they got back in their car, Jeff said to Kendra, "Your brother is the most irresponsible person I've ever met. I can't imagine someone wanting to live his life like that." Jeff took the passenger's seat and Kendra took the wheel, since he'd just sucked down three Guinnesses like they were water.

"Lex has low expectations," Kendra agreed. "If he'd gone to art school like he wanted to when he was a teenager, things would probably have turned out completely different. He gets really intense about something, and he talks a good game about how he's going to do it, and then it fizzles out. He was that way about art school, and he was even that way about Nicole. A few months ago he's ready to marry her and start a big, Catholic family, and now they're broken up. I don't know what his problem is; he has no follow-through. At least when I decided to go to school for business communications, I stuck with it, and I'm making a career out of it."

"You're a lot like your brother in some ways," Jeff said. "You were both spoiled growing up, and you both expect the world to come to you on a silver platter. Both of you need to get a lot more realistic and a lot more ambitious. But you're right about one thing: I've never seen Lex follow through on a single thing he's started in the years I've known him. He wanted to be a police officer like your dad, even went so far as to get the job application, but never filled it out. He was going to join the Air Force and never followed up on that."

"He never would have made it in the military," Kendra commented. "He likes to sleep late and hates being told what to do."

"I only hope if Adrienne really is pregnant, and the kid really is Lex's, his family doesn't become another thing he starts and then abandons."

"What do you mean, if Adrienne really is pregnant?"

Jeff shrugged. "It seems to me Adrienne has been after Lex as a boyfriend since before they moved in together. I doubt there's ever been a time when she wanted to be 'just friends' with him."

"Do you really think so?"

"You think I'm a pretty good judge of character, don't you?"

"You're a great judge of character, Jeff. Everything you predict is going to happen with people happens."

"I think my assessment of Adrienne is pretty accurate. I didn't say it in so many words, but I've been afraid of something like this since Lex and Adrienne said they were moving in together. I think she's trying to trap him."

"For his sake, and for Adrienne's, I hope you're wrong," Kendra said. "Trapping a man is such a sneaky, manipulative, underhanded, and not to mention desperate thing to do, it gives womankind a bad name."

"It's antifeminist," Jeff added.

Kendra laughed. "I don't think I've ever heard you use that word before."

"But it's accurate, isn't it? I mean, a woman should be strong enough to enter a partnership with a man on her own merits, if that's her choice, right?"

"You're right; it's just strange to hear you put it in those terms." They laughed at themselves for having a semantic discussion while Lex was having a crisis, but there was nothing more Kendra and Jeff could do about it.

Ten - To Catch a Liar
September, 2003

Jeff was in the middle of a large job, remodeling the guest bathroom, front entryway and kitchen for an older couple who lived in a condo on the far west side of the city. He'd assembled all the tools he would need for the day and loaded them into the van. Over the past few months, Jeff and the owner of the florist shop had come to an agreement regarding the parking. The florist gave Jeff and Kendra an easement, allowing them to remove part of the wall separating their property from the florist's lot. Jeff was then able to create a driveway in the back yard.

About to pull out of his driveway in the rear of the florist's lot, Jeff noticed a brown SUV with a code enforcement logo on the passenger door. Katherine Tate sat in the passenger seat. An elderly man drove. The vehicle sat at the stop sign at the end of Edgewater Drive, facing Jeff's house. Kate and the older man paused there for a few moments, talking and pointing at the house.

They must have noticed Jeff pulling out of his driveway. The code enforcement vehicle turned left, going south on the Cedar Street bridge. Jeff turned right out of the florist lot behind the vehicle, heading toward his job. He expected the code enforcement vehicle to turn off at town hall, yet they were still leading him in the direction he went.

The older man rolled down the driver's side window. He stuck his hand out and threw a candy wrapper backwards at Jeff's van. Jeff hated littering. Seeing a town employee not only litter, but also throw his litter at Jeff's van, pissed him off.

Jeff rolled down his window. "You son of a bitch!" he yelled, though he doubted the code enforcement officers could hear him as they disappeared from sight. As he pulled his head back into the vehicle, the wind blew Jeff's hat from his head. He pulled over and got out of the van to retrieve his hat before going on to work.

That day he laid ceramic tiles for the guest bath and entryway floors. At the end of the day, his back and knees ached from being bent over all day. Jeff left the job for the day at three that afternoon, when he couldn't lay any more tiles without cutting off the walkway.

He came home, took off his mortar-spattered clothes, and got in the shower. He sat on the couch to watch Oprah and drink a beer. First, though, he would call the mayor's office.

"Mayor Jonathon Thompson's office; this is Rachelle. How may I help you?"

"Rachelle, this is Jeffrey Gray. I spoke to you once before. I live on Cedar Street, and I want to talk to the mayor about some code enforcement employees. I saw them littering."

"The mayor's not in right now, Mr. Gray. Would you like to leave a message on his voice mail?"

"Yes," Jeff said. Rachelle transferred the call, and Jeff left a message: "Mayor Jonathon, this is Jeffrey Gray, in the big white house on Cedar Street, near the bridge. I was driving to work this morning behind two of your code enforcement officers. One of them was Katherine Tate. I don't know who the other one was, the one who was driving, but he was an elderly man. Anyway, as I was driving behind them, I saw the driver roll down his window and litter. If code enforcement officers are littering from city vehicles, it's a bad example for the rest of the town." Jeff left his phone number and asked the mayor to call him back.

When Kendra got home, Jeff told her about it. "That sucks," she said. "Nobody should be littering, but least of all people whose job it is to enforce city ordinances."

"Not only that, but when the guy flicked his candy wrapper at my vehicle, he was disrespecting me," Jeff said. "I didn't like the way they were looking at our house and pointing, either. A town government shouldn't be treating its citizens like that."

"They're bullies," Kendra agreed. "They get a little bit of power and they lord it over people, instead of remembering they work for the citizens. Not only do we pay their salaries, but they were specifically hired to be our servants."

"That's right," Jeff said. "That's the principle our country was founded on: the government works for the people, not the other way around. If these code enforcement officers can't remember that, I think it's time for Mayor Jonathon to replace them."

The next morning as he gathered his tools and job materials for the day, Jeff expected a call from Mayor Jonathon. It never came. Jeff stopped by town hall on his way to work to see if he could get the situation resolved. He went to into the code enforcement office.

At right before ten in the morning, town hall bustled with people. By chance, the elderly man who'd been driving the brown SUV stood behind the desk. "What's your name?" Jeff asked him.

"Why do you want to know?"

"Because I saw you littering yesterday."

"It wasn't me," the man said. "It must have been somebody else you saw."

"No," Jeff insisted. "It was you. I saw you and Kate Tate in a brown SUV with code lettering on the side. As we were headed south on Cedar, you rolled down your window and threw trash at my van." By then, every eye in the office was on Jeff and the old man.

"I did not," the old man insisted.

"You're a liar," Jeff said. "What's your name? I'm going to talk to the mayor about you."

The old man said, "I'm Earl McGhee, and I'm the head of code enforcement."

Jeff remembered Earl from phone conversations. He left the building and went to work. When he returned home at the end of the day and still hadn't received a phone call from Jonathon, Jeff dialed the mayor's office again. This time, he got the mayor on the line.

"Jonathon, this is Jeff Gray again. I called you yesterday afternoon about one of your code enforcement officers littering."

"I remember," Jonathon said. "I heard you were in the code enforcement office today."

"That's right," Jeff said. "I wanted to get my facts straight and find out the name of the man who was with Kate Tate yesterday. It was Earl McGhee, the head of code enforcement."

"Do you have any evidence?" the mayor asked him. "Did you happen to take any pictures? A video, maybe?"

"I wish I had," Jeff said, "but I didn't. I was driving. I wish my wife had been with me as a witness, but she was at work at the time."

"I'll look into it," Jonathon said. "At this point, all I have to go on is your word against Earl's and Katherine's. I'm not saying I don't believe you. You have had words with Katherine in the past, haven't you?"

"Yes," Jeff admitted. "The way she comes across is so disrespectful to citizens. Before I got behind the code enforcement vehicle in my van, Earl and Kate were sitting at the traffic sign on Edgewater Drive for at least a minute, not waiting for traffic, but sitting there, talking and pointing at my house. I couldn't hear what they were saying, but there's nothing about the front of my house that's any of their business."

"You're right, Mr. Gray," the mayor said. "I'll have a talk with Earl when I see him at our meeting tomorrow morning."

Jeff got off the phone, but he wasn't happy with the whole incident.

Every two weeks or so, Jeff and Kendra got a new letter from code enforcement, telling them their grass was too long and needed to be mowed. Even when the grass was trimmed short, they got letters about weeds in their yard. Jeff couldn't understand what weeds the letter referred to until he remembered the row of flowers Kendra had attempted to grow along the wall separating the house from the parking lot. She hadn't kept up with watering them and had discovered that side of the house didn't get much sunlight anyway. Soon the weeds took over.

Jeff thought these things over one Saturday morning as he mowed the lawn. The mail carrier came by. Jeff shut off his electric mower and took the mail from the carrier.

"Thanks," Jeff said to the carrier as he paged through the mail. He saw a letter from code enforcement. Again? he thought. He read the letter; it told him to mow his lawn. "God damn it!" Jeff said.

Tired of putting up with the constant bombardment of letters, Jeff went inside. He found Elizabeth Montoya's phone number and called the city councilor. To his surprise, she was home, and he got her on the phone.

"Elizabeth, this is Jeff Gray down the street."

"Jeff, how are you?" she said.

"I'm pissed off," he replied. "I was outside mowing my yard when the mailman came up and handed me a letter telling me to mow my yard. This has gotten past the point of them wanting to make sure my yard looks good. Now they're harassing me."

"Well, I don't understand. Usually, if the town has a problem with a property in my district, they'll come talk to me about it. I haven't heard a thing about your house. I didn't even notice your yard looking like it needed mowing."

"I know," Jeff said. "That's it exactly. I caught the head of code enforcement, Earl McGhee, littering out of his vehicle about a month and a half ago. He threw a candy wrapper out of his window at my van. He didn't like me catching him and they've been harassing me ever since. I even talked to the mayor, and nothing's been done about it."

"I'll see what I can do," she said.

After his conversation with Elizabeth, the letters stopped coming. Jeff let the grass get a little long to test the waters; still, no letter came from code. Jeff breathed a sigh of relief; Elizabeth seemed to have solved things.

Code enforcement faded to the back of Jeff's mind as family matters sprang up. Lex called Kendra one night in early October and asked her and Jeff for a favor. He needed "neutral ground" for a meeting between his parents and Adrienne's. Jeff and Kendra agreed, then hurried to complete a series of projects on the first floor of their home. Jeff and Kendra catered a dinner for the meeting families. Jeff made prime rib and salmon steaks and set out a huge buffet. The meeting could have been a disaster, but Jeff and Kendra pulled it off.

Eleven - Death's Day
December, 2011

The phone rang. Jeff picked it up and listened. Silence.

"Hello?" he heard on the other end."Hello, is somebody there?"

"What do you want?"

"This is Captain Michael Fisher with the St. Joseph County SWAT Team," the calm voice on the other end of the line replied."Am I speaking with Mr. Jeffrey Gray?"

"Yeah," Jeff spat."What do you want?"

"Mr. Gray, I want you to surrender. I want this whole thing to be over without anyone else getting hurt."

"This will all be over soon. I won't make you guys do anything. My father-in-law is a police officer, and I have nothing but respect for you guys. This isn't going to be a suicide-by-cop, but it will all be over in a little while."

"Mr. Gray, we'd like for everybody to walk out of there, including you."

"That's not going to happen," Jeff said. He wondered when, and how, he was finally going to end this. He knew he couldn't stay holed up in the burnt-out building forever, and though he knew the end was coming, he was still not looking forward to it.

"Mr. Gray, is the mayor there with you?"

Shit, Jeff thought. He didn't want the police to know the mayor had probably died. If they thought the mayor was dead, they had no reason to go easy on Jeff. If the fire department thought the mayor was dead, they'd probably take their axes to the doors and bust through Jeff's barriers, no longer afraid of endangering the mayor's safety.

Jeff shuffled his feet through the blood-stained papers on the floor and made some noise. "He's busy," Jeff said into the receiver. "I can take a message." He shuffled his feet some more. The blinds were still closed, so there was no way the police could see Jeff.

"Mr. Gray, what is it I can do for you?" Captain Fisher continued. "Is there something you want from the city? What are your demands? Why don't you tell me what they are, and we can talk about making some of those things happen for you."

Jeff paced the room. "I only have one demand: I want to tell my side of the story. Let me talk to the media. Get a reporter from the Willow Bend Tribune on the phone. Just make sure it's not that bitch Angela Singer."

"I'll see what we can do," Fisher said.

The next few moments were agonizing as Jeff had nothing to do but wait. He still smelled smoke, though he knew the fire department had already handled the blazing car. The carpet, drenched, squished as Jeff paced, it was as though he walked on a wet sponge. The water oozed up under his footsteps, black with carbon.

The explosion of the shotgun had ripped a hole in Jeff's cheek, right above his jaw that dripped blood and made him forget all about the slight puncture wound from the glass shard. It made it painful to talk, but Jeff was determined to get his story out no matter how much it hurt. His plans to make the mayor suffer may have been derailed, but at least the world would know why Jonathon had to suffer.

He knew from conversations with Wade the police wouldn't let him talk to the media. He knew he would have to contact them on his own. Jeff grew tired of waiting. He figured the cops were up to something. He'd been unable to call out on Jeff's office phone; the SWAT Team must have isolated the line.

He bent over Jonathon, reached inside Jonathon's jacket pocket, and found the mayor's Blackberry. It had been destroyed by a piece of buckshot when the shotgun exploded. He searched through the mayor's desk and found a cell phone…Jonathon's private cell phone. He scrolled through the mayor's contacts and found the number of a local television reporter whose name he recognized. He hit send, and to his surprise, the reporter answered.

"This is Sidney Broadbent."

"I've got an exclusive story for you," Jeff said.

"Jonathon?" Sidney asked. "That doesn't sound like you."

"My name is Jeff Gray."

"Mr. Gray, why are you calling me from the mayor's phone?"

"Because he's right here. I tried telling my story to the newspaper years ago. They skewed everything in the government's favor. Those goddamn editors don't care about the truth anymore. They only want to kiss the government's ass. Far be it from them to have to actually work for their material; they get it handed to them directly from the mayor's office."

"What are you talking about?" Sidney asked.

"Are you watching the news?" Jeff asked back. "Do you know what's going on in Princess City?"

"There's a fire or something at town hall," Sidney said. "Nobody seems to know what's going on."

"I'm what's going on!" Jeff said. "I'm at city hall right now. I'm in the mayor's office, in fact."

"Oh.   Oh! Let me get something to record this conversation, Jeff," Sidney encouraged him. "Let me get you on record."

"Hurry up; I don't have much time. Are you ready?"

"Okay, okay. I'm ready. For the record, state your name."

"I'm Jeff Gray."

"Okay, Jeff. What are you doing at city hall?"

"Well, I've driven my car through the building, set it on fire, and right now I'm holding the mayor hostage."

"What are you trying to accomplish?"

"I want the world to know the government shouldn't be allowed to take someone's home without a fight. A citizen should be able to fight for his own property, as if he were defending his own country."

"What, specifically, would you want the citizens to know?"

Jeff paused for a moment to get his words right. These words would give him the courage to go on.

"You guys have destroyed the fundamental values of the American system. Freedom of speech is so reporters have the ability to hold politicians accountable, so the people are protected from tyrants, so the people are not allowed to be bullied and taken advantage of.... Our system was not set up for the government to be able to do with a man's kingdom whatever they want. It was set up to protect that man's kingdom, to allow him to feel that his borders, no matter how great or small, would always be secure and that he would always be allowed to defend them. The Supreme Court took that right away with their eminent domain ruling back in 2005. The governments have taken advantage of that eminent domain ruling, and you, the media, have failed at protecting citizens. I tried to tell my side of the story to that bitch Angela Singer, and she skewed it in favor of the government and made me look like a fool. I worked so hard every day to keep my home and grow my kingdom, and these people just kept pouring salt in my wounds. What I've done today will make them think twice before they ever do it to a citizen again. The revolution is coming; I'm just planting the seeds. Everyone may not see it this way, but I'm a freedom fighter. They've tried to steal my freedom, and I'm paying for it with my life. One day, people will see my death was for their freedom, like the patriots in the American Revolution. That's it; that's all I wanted to say."

He paused. Sidney waited thirty seconds before saying, "Is there anything more you'd like to say, Mr. Gray?"

"No," he said. "If you don't do anything else with my last words, at least give them to my wife and tell her I love her."

Jeff hung up the phone and paced the room, thinking once again of how he would end things. He bent and picked up Jonathon's gun and looked it over. He took the clip out and popped out the one bullet still in the chamber. While it was empty, he stuck the barrel of the gun in his mouth and pulled the trigger, dry, just to see how it functioned. "I can do that," he told himself.

He guessed there were fourteen or fifteen bullets left in the clip as he reloaded the gun. He shot at the wooden double doors to see what it sounded like. Then he put the barrel between his lips and thought about it for a moment. He calculated where the bullet would come out. He didn't want to survive this. He wanted to make sure there would be no brain activity when the SWAT Team came in for him.

"I'm not ready," Jeff said. He put the gun on Jonathon's desk.

Jeff sat on the corner of the mayor's desk and picked up the cell phone. He called Kendra's cell. He wasn't sure he wanted her to answer the phone, but she picked up on the second ring. "Hello?" she said.

"Hi, baby, it's Jeff. What are you up to?"

"I'm on a break between conference sessions," she said. "I'm sitting by the hotel's fountain, sipping my coffee and watching the water."

"Sounds nice. I can hear the water in the background. Are you having a good time?"

"Yeah," she said. "It's not bad for a work-related conference. I'm meeting some interesting people from other magazines."

"Good," he said, wiping a tear from his eye. He was glad she was happy for the moment, blissfully ignorant of what was going on in her hometown. He hated to think of what would happen when she found out.

"How about you, Jeff?"

"I'm sore," he said. "I worked really hard today."

"Yeah, I can hear it in your voice," she said. "Maybe you should take some Tylenol and soak in the tub."

"I might do that," he said. It sounded wonderful, though he knew it was a pleasure he would never have again.

"Are you keeping yourself busy?"

"Yeah," he said, looking around at all the destruction. His face hurt like hell, and his feet were soaked with sooty water. "I've found a few things to do."

"What is that I hear in the background?"

"It's the PA system on the fire trucks; there was an accident on the far end of the bridge."

"I hope no one was hurt," she said. "Where are you calling me from? I didn't recognize the phone number."

"Huh," he said. "I don't know." He shrugged it off and hoped she wouldn't think too much about it. "Kendra, I won't keep you too much longer, but I want you to know I love you and I miss you."

"I love you, too," she said. "And I miss you, too. I wish you were here."

"I wish I was, too. Bye, baby."

"Bye, sweetie pie. I'll see you Saturday."

As he hung up, he thought that Kendra wouldn't see him on Saturday. He paced around the mayor's office once again. He paused in front of the window, separated the blinds, and peered out.

This wasn't how it was supposed to be. Jeff's life was supposed to end on the beach in Florida or Hawaii, not slogging through the burnt-out hull of the town hall with the dead mayor at his feet. Jeff had dreams of selling the house and retiring with money in his bank account and little responsibility. He always thought he'd like to own a hot dog cart and push it around the beach all day, selling hot dogs and pop, to the tourists and beach bums and ogling the girls in their bikinis. Oh, the girls, he thought. He would come up with his own proprietary blends of mustard and relish, and everyone on the beach would know Jeff and his hot dogs. He dreamed of calling it "Beach Dogs."

It was a dream he'd shared with Kendra many times during their happier moments. Kendra even had a dream of her own: she would follow behind Jeff's hot dog cart in a tricycle outfitted with baskets on the front and sides. She'd fill them with books, magazines, and newspapers, and ride around the beach buying, selling and trading reading material. By then, Jeff and Kendra would be very old. She'd already have retired from her newspaper job, where she'd been an honest-to-God reporter and not just a layout designer for years. She'd probably have won a Pulitzer Prize by then.

Jeff shed a few tears as he thought about Kendra. He'd only wanted to protect her, to grow old with her, to provide her with the home of her dreams. It wasn't supposed to end like this. This wasn't the story Jeff was supposed to have written for himself. It hurt Jeff's heart to think about what he was doing to Kendra. For that reason, he'd waited until she was gone before doing what he felt he needed to do.

Twelve - Apology
Late September, 2003

Jeff and Kendra finished the major demolition on the house. They'd torn off the old, green roof and worked on finishing the new, blue-gray roof. The trash trailer was twenty five feet long and was getting in the way more than it was helping now, so Jeff decided to sell it. He moved it from the back driveway to the front of the house, parking it on the grass with only the tongue extending onto the concrete parking pad, and put a "For Sale" sign on the front. He didn't block any part of the sidewalk. Even though Elizabeth Montoya had taken care of things with code enforcement, Jeff tried not to do anything that would bring attention to his house.

Two days after Jeff put the trailer up for sale, he received a letter from code enforcement. "What does it say?" Kendra asked him, attempting to read the letter over Jeff's shoulder.

"That I can't have my trailer in the yard because it's blocking the sidewalk," Jeff replied.

Kendra walked over to the dining room and looked out the window. "It's nowhere near the sidewalk," she said. "It's hardly even over the parking pad, but that's our property anyway."

"I'll call them and see if I can get this straightened out," Jeff said, knowing the town was singling him out again. He called town hall, connected with the code enforcement office and spoke with Earl McGhee.

"I was careful not to block the sidewalk specifically for this reason," Jeff told Earl. "I knew you guys were going to give me shit, and you did."

"Jeff, you're not allowed to have your trailer parked on the grass," Earl told him. "Forget about the sidewalk. If you park your vehicle on your lawn, and I let you get away with it, pretty soon everybody's going to start parking their cars on their lawns and the whole town's going to look like trash."

"How the hell am I supposed to sell my trailer if it isn't parked in the front of my house?" Jeff argued. "No one's going to see it in the back."

"We can't make an exception for you," Earl insisted. "You get that thing off the grass, and then you can worry about how you're going to sell it."

Jeff hung up. "God damn bastards," he shouted. "Fucking pieces of shit."

"What's wrong?" Kendra asked.

"I have to go move the god damn trailer," Jeff said. He took the camera outside with him and took some pictures of where the trailer sat. He wanted proof it wasn't blocking the sidewalk.

He went outside and hooked up the van, then moved the trailer. Now, instead of the grass, the entire thing rested on the parking pad. It covered the whole pad and looked rather awkward, since the parking pad had been designed for an average-sized car, but it didn't block the public sidewalk. Another two days went by, and Jeff received a second letter from code enforcement telling him he couldn't block the sidewalk with his trailer.

Furious, Jeff called Earl's office again. Without even waiting for a salutation, he began, "I'm not blocking the god damn sidewalk and I'm not parked on the god damn grass. My trailer is on the concrete parking pad on my private property. What the hell do you people want from me?"

Earl chuckled. "Jeff, we've received a series of complaints about that vehicle parked in your front yard."

"From who?" Jeff demanded. "I could drive around the city and point out to you a dozen or more other trailers parked in people's front yards that really are blocking the sidewalk, and I bet you those owners aren't being given the same kind of harassment you're giving me."

"We're only doing what the city attorney has asked us to do," Earl said.

"Then let me talk to him."

"The city attorney's a her, not a him. I'll transfer you." He waited for a moment, and a woman picked up the phone.

"This is Justine Ernsberger," she said.

"Justine, are you the city attorney?"

"Yes."

"My name is Jeffrey Gray. I live at the house on Cedar Street next to the bridge."

"I'm familiar with that house," Justine said. Jeff didn't like the disdainful way she said it.

"Maybe you're also familiar with the problem I've been having with code enforcement," he continued. "I have a trash trailer I'm trying to sell. I don't want the damn thing anymore, so I'm trying to get it out of my yard. In order to sell it, I need to have it out near my front yard where people can see it as they drive by. Code enforcement keeps sending me letters telling me I can't have a trailer in the front of my house, but I can't get rid of the trailer unless it's parked in front of my house. I'm not blocking the sidewalk, and I'm not parked on the grass. I don't know what the hell else to tell them. If this city doesn't start leaving me alone, I'm going to do something drastic to my house. If they think it's ugly with flaking paint on the awning and a trailer on the parking pad, wait 'til they see it pink with purple polka dots, and a giant hand flipping off the city painted on the side! I'm not going to put up with you guys doing this! I'll go to war with you guys."

"Mr. Gray," Justine interrupted, "I think you should know you've already had a police report filed against you."

"What?" Jeff yelled, astounded. "I haven't done anything."

"That's not what I heard, Mr. Gray. Mr. McGhee and Mrs. Tate from code enforcement told me you chased them at a high rate of speed across town, so I had them file a report with the police."

"I can't believe the nerve of you guys!" Jeff roared. "I wasn't chasing them, I was going to work. We went the same direction for all of four blocks, and it was not at a high rate of speed. They were the ones who broke the law; I caught them littering. They're pissed because I caught them! I want to know who's filing all these complaints against me."

"I am," Justine said. "I have to drive by your house every day on my way to work."

Jeff hung up on her, seething with rage. "Rotten bitch," he muttered. Jeff went into a rant, uttering every horrible word he could think of, linked together in rhythmic chains.

It was obvious the town wasn't going treat him fairly when the town's attorney herself conspired with code enforcement against him. He and Kendra were being harassed on the town attorney's whims, over her own personal tastes. Sure, the house wasn't finished and the yard wasn't landscaped. If Justine Ernsberger could see how much they'd already improved the inside, and how much more work they had to go, she would understand why they hadn't had time to get to the outside yet. The selling of the trailer, though, was none of her damn business. Jeff didn't know who to call first, the mayor or a lawyer. He was still cussing about it when Kendra came home from work.

"Fuck 'em," Jeff said to Kendra. "I'm leaving the god damn thing there. It's going to sell, and they can keep bitching at me."

She took off her shoes, then came over to where Jeff stood, staring out the windows at the river. She put her arms around him and kissed him. "What's the matter?" she asked him.

"It turns out it's the town's attorney, some bitch named Justine Ernsberger, who keeps complaining to code enforcement about our trailer," he said.

"That can't be good," Kendra said, slipping her arm around Jeff's waist and staring out at the river with him. ""They just don't want us to live here, do they?"

"No, they don't," Jeff said. "I guess they dreamed of some rich couple coming in here and restoring the house to its former glory in the blink of an eye."

"Is there anything we can do?"

"I'll talk to the mayor tomorrow," Jeff said. "If I can't get them to leave us alone after that, I'm going to call a lawyer. This is ridiculous."

"I'm sorry," Kendra said. "I'm sorry you have to deal with this bullshit while I'm at work. I'm sorry I talked you into buying this house when it's been nothing but trouble since the day we moved in."

"It's not the house's fault," Jeff reminded her. "I love this house. I love living near the parks, and I love living on the river. The problem is the town government. They're a bunch of petty tyrants who think working for a small-town government means they have the right to treat people like they don't matter. Well, I'm a citizen, and I matter. You're a citizen, and you matter."

"You tell 'em, Jeff."

"I will," he said. "Right now, though, let's go make some supper."

At this late afternoon hour, he would have to wait for the next day to do anything about it. After supper, Jeff and Kendra went for a walk in the park. They walked in the parks almost daily. When they'd first met, Central Park consisted of little more than a fishing spot, the driveway paved with stones instead of asphalt. Over the last few years, the town completely renovated it, with a new tennis court, a baseball diamond, and a pedestrian bridge that crossed over to the peninsula where the town's police station sat. Because the bridge looked out over a natural waterfall, it was a beautiful spot.

Battell Park lay on the other side of Main Street from Central Park about a half mile west of the house. The town planned to connect the two with a walkway under the Main Street Bridge on the north side of the river. On the south side, they began building a new park, named in honor of Mayor Thompson's predecessor, Al Stewart, who had been mayor for over twenty years.

The new park sat on an artificial island, created by a series of channels and waterfalls. It rivaled Willow Bend's raceway, but while the raceway was functional and used for kayaking events, the town's artificial branch of the river was purely ornamental. Still a year away from being completed, the park was encircled by fences, but Jeff and Kendra snuck around the fences and checked out the progress. Eventually, the city would have a river walk connecting all three parks and extending a mile and a half west to the Logan Street Bridge.

"Wasn't our real estate agent's husband a lawyer?" Kendra asked as they walked through Central Park.

"Yeah," Jeff said, "but he's not going to be any good to us. He's in tight with the local Republican Party, and he's not going to stand up to Justine."

Jeff couldn't get the town attorney out of his mind for the next few days, but he was too busy with work to give it his full attention. At night, though, he had trouble sleeping. He couldn't stop thinking about the injustice of the way the town was singling his house out for harassment. He tried taking melatonin and watching boring news programs in the middle of the night, but nothing seemed to get the thoughts of the town attorney out of his mind. He was becoming obsessed.

One evening, when he was sure she would already be home from the bank, Jeff called Elizabeth. "Hello?" she said.

Jeff launched into the story of the trailer and how code enforcement wouldn't leave him alone, even though he'd had no problems with them for months.

"Hold on a moment, Jeff," Elizabeth said. "There's something you should know: your side of Cedar Street is no longer in my district."

"What do you mean?" he asked.

"The town redrew the districting lines for the town council, and now I represent only the east side of North Cedar Street," she said. "You have a different councilor now."

"Who?"

"I'd be happy to see what I can do for you, but in the future you'll have to call Tim Rozniak."

When he relayed this bit of information to Kendra, she said, "You know, a more paranoid person might think she had the line redrawn on purpose so she didn't have to listen to our complaints anymore."

"You mean so she didn't have to listen to my complaints," Jeff said. "I didn't think I was a paranoid person, but now that the town attorney's confessed she's the one who's reporting us to code enforcement, I'm starting to wonder. It's not paranoia when they really are out to get you."

Finally, when the latest letter from code enforcement arrived, informing Jeff he couldn't park in front of his house and had two days to move the trailer, Jeff called the mayor's office. Rachelle answered and passed the phone call to Jonathon, who asked Jeff to talk directly to Justine. Jonathon transferred the phone to the attorney's office.

"I want a copy of the ordinance you say I'm violating," Jeff told Justine. "I want to show it to my attorney."

"Let me get back with you," she said. "I'll call you right back."

Jeff assented, thinking he would be lucky if he didn't have to hunt her down for days on end to get a response out of her. It surprised him when she called back fifteen minutes later.

"Mr. Gray, it seems your trailer will be fine where it is," Justine said. "I looked at the statute, and after further review, it turns out it only applies to motorized vehicles. Since your trailer has no motor, the statute doesn't apply to it."

"So you've been harassing me for two weeks, and I haven't even done anything wrong?"

"You have a good day, Mr. Gray." She hung up.

Jeff called the mayor's office and said, "I want to speak with Jonathon."

Rachelle transferred the call. "Jonathon, I just got off the phone with the city attorney, and she says the ordinance doesn't apply to my trailer. That means the whole time they've been harassing me about my trailer, I wasn't even doing anything wrong. They have intimidated me, threatened me, and filed a false police report against me. They have just plain been bullying me, all for nothing but their own gratification. I want a letter of apology. You wouldn't believe how many sleepless nights I've had over this. This is exhausting me. It wasn't until I said I wanted to show the ordinance to my attorney that they admitted I was right in the first place. How can you let these people run our town? This is your responsibility. If they're treating me like this, when I don't take shit off anybody, I can only imagine what they do to weaker citizens."

Jonathon said, "I apologize, Mr. Gray. It's our goal to take care of our citizens in the most fair and ethical manner possible. I'm sure if you were mistreated, it was unintentional. It was simply a misunderstanding about the ordinance."

"I expect to see a letter of apology," Jeff said. "I want to see the names of Katherine Tate, Earl McGhee, and Justine Ernsberger on the letter. All of them are culpable in this."

"I'll do that for you, Mr. Gray," the mayor said. "Again, I apologize for any inconvenience. You have a good day, Mr. Gray."

The letter arrived in the mail one week later.

Thirteen - The Offer
June, 2004

Late one morning, Jeff and Kendra lay in bed, her head resting on his bare chest. Jeff had an idea. "Kendra," he said, "how would you feel about asking your brother, Adrienne and the baby to move in with us?"

She yawned. "I don't know," she said. "It would be strange, I guess. Why?"

"Because when Lex worked for me, he was a good helper, once he showed up. There were days when he didn't have a lot of energy because he'd been out drinking the night before, but there were also days when he worked quicker and knew what he was doing better than you."

As they walked through the park that afternoon, Jeff and Kendra debated the pros and cons of asking Lex and Adrienne to move in with them. "Pro: we'd live in the same house as our niece, so we'd get to spend a lot more time with her," Kendra said.

"I do like the sound of that," Jeff agreed. "At this point, we're lucky if we get to see Rose once a month. Con: there would be a small child in the house. I'm sure Rose can be noisy at times. I wouldn't be able to sleep through it if she was up all night crying. Con: your brother is a smoker, and the house would stink like cigarettes. We'd have to paint again when Lex moved out."

"You mean Lex would have to repaint," Kendra said. "Besides, we don't have to allow him to smoke in the house. He could go outside; he does it at work all the time. Pro: Lex and Adrienne would be helping us get the house finished."

"Con: Lex is notorious for saying he's going to do something, and not following through. Con: I'm going to get pissed off if he screws around and doesn't get any work done on the place. Con: if I have to kick him, Adrienne and the baby out of the house, it's going to cause a huge rift in the family. Everyone's going to blame me, especially your mother. You know she always stands up for Lex, even when he does something incredibly stupid."

"That's true," Kendra admitted. "I've seen my mother get awfully angry with Lex, and yet still defend him whenever someone outside the family tried to criticize him."

"If something happens and we have to ask Lex and Adrienne to move, then I'm going to be called the heartless bastard who threw a mom and baby out of their home."

Jeff got called a heartless bastard before, in his landlord days, when he evicted a family.

"Pro: if nothing goes wrong, and we all live together happily, not only will the house get done quicker, but we'll score some brownie points with my mom for helping out my little brother."

They debated it for the next couple of days, and in the end, decided to call Lex and ask him, Adrienne and Rose to come over one evening that week. Jeff opened a bottle of wine and poured a glass for everyone. They sat in the second-floor living room, on the sectional couch, while Rose played with Kendra's old stuffed animals.

Before Jeff and Kendra could get to their proposal, Adrienne surprised them with some news of her own. "Lex got a new job," she said. "He's the new assistant manager at Cloverfield's East."

"Congratulations," Kendra said. "You'll be working right downtown, then, only a few blocks from here."

Cloverfield's East was a stone's throw from the new park. Jeff and Kendra went there two or three times a week to have a beer while out on their evening walks. "That's exciting, going from bartender to assistant manager."

"Yeah," Lex said. "I desperately needed a better-paying job. We were barely making it at the apartment. Diapers and formula add up quickly, and Rose outgrows her clothes faster than we can wash them."

"I'm glad you mentioned that," Jeff said. "Your sister and I were thinking of a way you and Adrienne could save some money, and help us out at the same time."

"What is it?" Adrienne asked.

"Move in here," Jeff said. "Instead of paying us rent in cash, you could work for your rent by helping us finish our house. Kendra and I are tired of living in a construction zone. We're ready to get settled in here and start handling other projects."

"I don't know," Lex said as he finished his glass of wine.

"Take some time to think about it," Jeff told them. "If I were you, Lex, I'd sit down with your dad, have a long talk with him and get his opinion."

"That's what I'll do," Lex agreed.

Jeff said, "You'd have to be really diligent about it. If you were living here and not paying us any rent, and you were supposed to be getting the house done, but you got too busy with the baby, or work, or whatever, Kendra and I would feel like you were taking advantage of us."

"That wouldn't happen, though," Lex insisted. "You would be saving us so much money by letting us live here, we'd make sure you were taken care of. If, for some reason, we were ever too busy to get our share of the work done, we'd pay you cash that month. We can work out all the details, though, if and when Adrienne and I do decide to move in."

Two weeks later, Lex and Adrienne knocked on Jeff and Kendra's door. It was a Monday evening. Kendra was in the kitchen getting supper ready. Jeff answered the door.

"This is a surprise," he said. "Come in. Where's the baby?"

"My mom and dad are watching her tonight," Adrienne said. "We just got done watching a movie. This is the first time we've been out of the house together since Rose was born."

"So what's up?" Jeff asked. "Can I get you a beer?"

"No, thanks," Lex said.

"We want to do that thing with you guys where we work for rent," Adrienne said.

Kendra came out of the kitchen, oven mitts still on her hands. "Hey, guys," she said. "I'd invite you to stay for supper, but I only made enough for Jeff and me."

"That's okay," Adrienne said. "We ate a load of popcorn at the theater, and weren't going to stay long anyway. We only wanted to tell you we want to move in."

"That's great," Kendra said.

"Did you talk it over with your dad?" Jeff asked him.

"No," Lex said. His answer surprised Jeff. He couldn't understand why Lex wouldn't go to his own father to talk about something so important. Jeff had a hard time figuring out the relationship between those two.

"How soon do you want to move in?" Jeff asked them.

"Well, our lease is up in a month," Adrienne said.

"Okay," Jeff said, "we're going to sign a lease and have everything spelled out so there's no confusion. Let's get together this weekend, and I'll have a lease ready." Lex and Adrienne agreed.

That Sunday, they got together once again in the second floor living room. "I want you to understand, cleaning your living space and taking care of the part of the house that is your home is not part of your rent labor," Jeff told them. "I expect you to keep your part of the house clean. I'll credit you for cleaning up messes that relate directly to construction work."

All four agreed Lex and Kendra's rent would consist of ten hours of work on the house per week. They calculated that at ten dollars an hour, rent would be a hundred dollars a week in the event Lex and Adrienne were unable to get their remodeling work done to the house.

"No problem," Lex said. "That's only five hours a week, or one hour a day, Monday through Friday, for each of us."

"It'll be really easy since we'll be living here," Adrienne agreed. "I'll want this stuff done quickly anyway."

"You'll have to keep track of what hours you work," Jeff told them. "I want to see documentation: what you did, when you started, and when you stopped. Basically, you need to make yourself a time card. I'd like to have you get your first week paid in advance. Come by next week and expect to put in ten hours."

"I'll be excited to live here," Lex said. "Our apartment is pretty small for the three of us. This way, we'll have extra room to spread out in."

"You can also use the basement for storage," Jeff said, knowing Lex alone came with an enormous collection of comic books, movies, and superhero action figures, the remaining fragments of his dreams of being a cartoonist.

After working on the house for the first two weeks, for a total of twenty hours, Lex and Adrienne sat on the back porch, smoking cigarettes, while Kendra played with Rose in the back yard. Jeff stood beside the porch with a beer in his hand.

"This is going to be exciting," Adrienne said. "I'm glad we get to be part of this house. It's a good feeling."

"It's cool to see it getting done," Lex agreed. "We're going to like living next door to you guys, too. We've seen each other more these last two weeks than ever before."

"Getting ten hours a week of work done is going to be a snap," Adrienne continued. "It really doesn't seem like it took up that much of our time."

"I hope you guys take this seriously, because I'm not going to be a pushover," Jeff told them. "Business and family don't normally mix, so we have to be diligent to make sure we don't screw this up. Do you guys understand?"

"Yes, we understand," Adrienne said. "Trust me, Jeff, we take this as seriously as you do." Jeff had a rule not to trust someone who said, "Trust me!" He ignored it.

After two weeks, Lex and Adrienne moved in with their baby. Adrienne's parents helped them by buying new appliances and furniture. The next time Jeff saw Lex, he asked him, "You got those paint chips cleaned off the floor before you moved the baby's crib in, right? There could be lead in that."

"I vacuumed in there," Lex said.

"Did you clean the floor with a damp sponge afterward?"

"No," Lex admitted.

"You should at least do that," Jeff told him. "Your baby's going to be crawling around in there."

Lex sighed. "I'll take care of it," he said.

In the meanwhile, Jeff and Kendra built themselves a kitchen upstairs, in the small bedroom facing the florist shop. Lex and Adrienne would then be able to demolish the first floor's back kitchen and, with Jeff and Kendra's help, turn it into a decent bedroom.

One day, after he and Kendra had been in the downstairs apartment to drop off a gift for Rose, Jeff noticed a mess of drywall chunks near the stairway door separating their apartments. Lex and his family weren't home at the time, but Jeff called Adrienne later. "Would you clean up that drywall mess in your bedroom?" he asked her. "I'll apply it toward your rent time."

"Okay," Adrienne said. She got off the phone.

Several days later, Jeff noticed the drywall debris still lying near the stairway. He knocked on the side door. When Adrienne came to the door, Jeff told her, "I asked you to clean that mess up. I'm not in the habit of repeating myself; now please get it done." He went back upstairs.

Moments later, Jeff got a phone call from Lex. "What the hell's going on? Why am I getting phone calls at work from Adrienne, crying, saying you're being mean to her?"

"What are you talking about?" Jeff asked Lex. "I asked her to clean up the mess of drywall in your bedroom. I paid close attention to my tone of voice and chose my words carefully."

"That's not what Adrienne said," Lex continued. "I don't have time for this shit, Jeff. I can't deal with this right now." He hung up.

Jeff explained the phone call to Kendra. "I'm confused," he said. "I don't have any idea what I possibly could have said to her to make her call up Lex at work, bawling. I wasn't disrespectful. Maybe she's upset because of her post-pregnancy hormones. She might have post-partum depression."

"I should talk to her about it," Kendra said.

"I don't know," Jeff said. "I don't know if we should say anything to them or not. You'd better at least wait until your brother gets home from work."

Jeff called Adrienne's mobile phone and left an apology on her voice mail to help smooth things over with her. He could already see trouble brewing.

That summer, for Wade's birthday, Adrienne organized a family dinner at Cloverfield's East. Lex would be working while the Wilsons and the Newtons arrived for the party. Jeff and Kendra bought Wade a gift box of Jack Daniels, with two rocks glasses, and wrapped a red ribbon around it. The gray clouds threatened rain. Though Jeff and Kendra could have walked to the restaurant, they decided to drive. Jeff pulled into the parking lot and looked for a space when he saw Mayor

Jonathon Thompson, dressed in a dark blue suit, walking toward the restaurant.

"That's the mayor," Kendra said.

"Yeah," Jeff said. He grabbed Kendra's hand and hurried toward the door, frantic to talk to the mayor before he walked into the restaurant. With her other hand, Kendra clutched her father's birthday gift to her chest.

"Mayor Jonathon," Jeff said loudly. The mayor turned around. "I assume you know who I am."

"No," Jonathon responded.

"I'm Jeffrey Gray; I live across the bridge from town hall, on Cedar St."

A look of recognition dawned on Jonathon's face. "Yes, I'm familiar with your house," Jonathon said.

"May I talk to you for a moment?" Jeff asked.

Jonathan said, "Sure; I've got just a minute."

"Your administration is causing me a lot of frustration with my home. They're micromanaging my property and I can't take it much more. I used to love this city. I wanted to move back to this town because I believed it was a safe place to be. Your de facto first lady of the city, Justine Ernsberger, is causing me all kinds of problems with my property." Jeff had learned Jonathon and Justine were dating. "She has Earl and Kate acting like her lap dogs, and they won't quit harassing me. I get done mowing my yard, and I have a letter in my mailbox telling me to mow my yard. I bet you still haven't done anything about Earl littering. I knew he was going to lie to you. How can you let these people get away with treating your citizens like this? It's going to come back and bite you if you don't do something about it."

Justine came walking around the corner. "There you are," she said. "I was looking for you."

Jeff didn't miss a beat. "And you!" he said. "If you hadn't lied in the first place, none of this would have happened. You leave my property alone."

Jeff and Kendra turned and walked into the rear entrance of the restaurant, while the mayor and the town attorney went to the front.

The hostess took the mayor and the town attorney to a table on the main floor. Lex greeted his sister and Jeff and took them up the stairs to the mezzanine, where Adrienne and Rose, Wade and Candace, and Adrienne's parents Kirk and Eileen waited for them. Jeff took a seat across from Wade as Kendra put the box of Jack down among the gifts on the far side of the table. At the other end, Rose in her high chair smashed packets of crackers under the palms of her hands.

"Happy birthday, sir," Jeff said as he sat down.

"Thank you," Wade said.

"I just ran into the mayor outside," Jeff continued. "He and I had a nice little chat."

"Just now?" Wade said.

"Yeah," Kendra piped in. "The mayor and the city attorney are having dinner right below us."

"Well, don't turn around and spit in his soup," Wade said. "I'd hate for Lex to have to kick us out of this place."

"Had some troubles with the mayor, have you?" Kirk asked. Jeff told him about some of his experiences with the town government as the server arrived to take their drink orders. By the time the salads arrived, Jeff had almost forgotten about it...but not quite. Wade's birthday dinner was a happy occasion, and Jeff never got tired of the Pittsburgh-style steak at Cloverfield's.

"I can't get the mayor and the city attorney out of my head," Jeff told Kendra as he tried to sleep that night. This was turning into a common complaint for him. A week after Wade's birthday party, Jeff went to his family doctor and admitted he had obsessive thoughts about the town government and its unfairness.

"Would you say these thoughts interfere with your day-to-day activities?" the doctor asked.

"Yes," Jeff said. "Once I start thinking about it at night, I can't sleep. I wake up early in the morning and think about it some more. Is there anything I can do about it?"

"We can try you out on a prescription antidepressant," the doctor said. Jeff and Kendra had done some research on antidepressants, and after the doctor gave Jeff a few choices, Jeff chose the one that seemed to have the smallest number of side effects. He'd never thought of himself as someone who needed medication, but after a few weeks went by, he did notice he was losing less sleep thinking about the city. He didn't know if it was a placebo effect or if the medicine was making a difference; either way, he was happy to move on and turn the page.

After a couple of months, Lex and Adrienne started paying the rent in cash, one hundred dollars a week, instead of working on the house. This made Jeff unhappy, but he understood they had a lot of responsibility on their shoulders. He decided to let them get away with it, without saying anything.

Over those same few months, Lex and Adrienne didn't get along very well. Jeff and Kendra could hear them arguing late into the night, when Lex came home. One morning, Lex called Kendra and said, "Adrienne and I have decided to separate."

"What?" she said. "Why would you need to separate when you aren't even, technically, together?"

"It's hard living with someone," Lex said. "You and Jeff are lucky. You love each other, and you're compatible, so it's easier for you to share a home. I'm jealous of you guys."

"I wouldn't exactly call it easy," Kendra said. "We're kind of an odd couple. He's picky about certain things, and I'm lazy and sloppy. Still, we manage to work it out somehow…and you and Adrienne have Rose to think about."

"You would think that'd make it easier, but Adrienne and I have reached the point where we can't live together anymore. I asked her to leave."

Kendra was silent for a moment. Then she said, "Whatever you think is best, Lex. Does she have somewhere to go?"

"Yeah," Lex said. "Her sister Monique just built a new modular home on some land Kirk and Eileen own, out by the farm. Monique told Adrienne she could stay in the basement. Kirk and some of Adrienne's cousins are going to help her get it finished really quickly."

"Is she taking Rose with her?"

"We're going to share responsibilities. I'll have her some of the time and Adrienne will have her some of the time.

We already have a schedule worked out. Of course, we'll use the two sets of grandparents to help us out, too."

"That's too bad," Kendra said, "but I'm sure you felt like it had to be done."

Kendra relayed the news to Jeff, who called Lex. "I sympathize with you, Lex," Jeff said. "I do feel bad for you, going through a tough time in your life. On the other hand, this means you're going to have to carry the whole load of the forty hours a month now. Because you and Adrienne decided to split up doesn't mean I need your help any less."

"It's not going to be a big deal," Lex said. "I can do ten hours a week, or at least a hundred dollars. I'm on board."

Whether he meant it at the time or not, Lex might as well have lied. Time passed, and Lex seemed to get depressed. Jeff saw no reason to let Lex free from his responsibility of helping with the house and continued to call Lex and give him things to do. Soon Lex stopped answering Jeff's phone calls. Jeff became furious.

"How could he be such a god damn coward that he can't even talk to me? I'm not going to put up with this much longer," Jeff said to Kendra. "He comes in late at night, slamming doors and waking me up. You know how hard it is for me to get back to sleep."

One day while he was at work, steaming mad, Jeff called Lex

and told him, "In order to save the family, you get your shit and you get the fuck out of my house by the end of this week."

After days of angry phone calls to Kendra questioning how Jeff could do this to him, Lex turned to Adrienne's parents for help. They accepted him, coming by with a moving truck to help Lex get his furniture and appliances out of the Grays' house.

"Where will you go?" Kendra asked her brother.

Lex sighed. "Adrienne is a bigger person than I am. She said I could stay with her in Monique's walk-out basement until we can get a place of our own."

"I thought you and Adrienne couldn't live together anymore."

"I thought so, too," Lex said.

For three weeks, the Grays didn't communicate with Adrienne and Lex. Then Lex answered one of Kendra's phone calls and agreed to meet Kendra and Jeff in the park. Kendra and Lex sat in the park and talked while Jeff picked up lunch from a fast-food restaurant on Lincoln Way, about a mile west of downtown.

Jeff arrived with a bag full of tacos, and as they ate, Jeff told Lex, "I can't believe the way you disrespected me and my house. You tried to take advantage of me, but more importantly, you tried to take advantage of your sister. In your mind, because you're depressed about all your responsibilities, she's supposed to let you live here forever for free. I can't believe your sense of entitlement. Kendra's the same way sometimes; it must have something to do with the way you were raised."

"Don't say anything about my mom and dad," Lex began.

"Don't you dare get defensive with me," Jeff countered. "You're the one who tried to screw us here. As for getting thrown out of the house, you got what you deserved, whether you see it that way or not. I love you, Lex, but I'm not going to put up with infinite shit from you. That's not how family members treat each other; that's how a parasite treats its host, taking and never giving. You should be ashamed for taking advantage of your sister. If you ever disrespect me like that again, I won't have anything to do with you."

"I'm sorry," Lex said to Kendra. "I'm sorry, Jeff. I didn't mean to disrespect you or your house."

"I understand you have a lot of responsibilities with your baby," Jeff said, "but we have a lot of responsibilities with this house. If we don't get this house done, we'll be financially ruined. That house is our child."

"I wasn't thinking about it like that," Lex said. "I wasn't thinking."

The talk made both sides feel better about things. Then Jeff and Lex got along better than ever.

Fourteen - Family Time
November, 2005

Over the summer, Jeff decided to turn the back living room, that Lex used for a bedroom, into a kitchen for the first floor. He and Kendra recycled a sink and countertops from one of his customers. They picked up an inexpensive set of scratch-and-dent appliances and soon had a beautiful new kitchen.

"Maybe it's time we have the whole family over," Jeff told Kendra when the kitchen was finished.

Kendra looked around. "Do you think we're ready?"

Jeff laughed. "Why don't you tell your family we're going to have Thanksgiving here?"

Kendra agreed. They told Wade and Candace about it, and they in turn notified Lex, along with Kendra's aunts and uncles.

On Thanksgiving Day, Jeff and Kendra woke up at four to put the turkey in the oven, then went back to bed. "I'm nervous," Kendra confessed as they lay down. "I've never cooked for this many people before. I've never even had this many people over to a house I've lived in before; when my mom's parents were still alive, they hosted these things."

"You'll do fine," Jeff assured her. "The turkey will cook itself, and I'll carve it. You'll be responsible for the mashed potatoes and the vegetables, and that's about it, right? Your mom and your Aunt Florence are making the rest, aren't they?"

"Yeah," she said. "I guess you're right."

He put his arm around her. "Of course, if you're really too nervous to get back to sleep, there are other things we can do." Kendra giggled and rolled onto her side. They kissed and made love. Jeff soon fell asleep.

Later that morning, Candace and Wade arrived first, followed by Uncle Alex and Aunt Florence. Alex and Florence's teenage daughter, Cheyenne, stood behind them, her arms loaded with plastic containers of food. They all arrived loaded down with food.

Jeff regarded the last-minute preparations with amusement. He helped arrange the buffet table in the first-floor kitchen. Wade and Jeff brought the extra chairs in from the back of Candace's SUV and arranged them around the dining room table. After he'd taken the turkey out of the oven, Jeff carved the bird and set the serving tray on the edge of the buffet. "Okay, everybody, let's eat!" he announced.

By then, Lex and Adrienne had arrived, with Rose in tow. "Wow," Adrienne said as she looked around, "I can hardly believe this is the same house! You painted Rose's room!"

"Yeah," Kendra said. "I could've put up with the aqua, but Jeff wanted a more subdued color for the office."

"And the French doors are gone," Lex added.

"It broke my heart to get rid of those," Jeff said. "They were falling apart, though."

The last guests to arrive were Ellis Cho and Sun Park. Sun's family didn't celebrate Thanksgiving. Ellis had lost her mother earlier in the year, and didn't have any living relatives in town. Kendra and Jeff were busy in the upstairs kitchen when they arrived.

Sun and Ellis wandered into the upstairs kitchen. He took a bottle of Blue Moon from the fridge and snaked his arm around Ellis's waist.

"Good choice," Jeff said, pointing to Sun's beer. "This Guinness is awful stuff, just awful." Jeff took a gulp from the Guinness in his hand.

"I see you like Guinness," Sun said.

"Just a little," Jeff replied.

The family stayed and talked long after they'd eaten, had seconds, picked at the leftovers and finished off the pies. Jeff and Kendra got concerned about food safety and put the remaining leftovers away. The relatives upstairs played spades with some decks of cards Jeff had left on the windowsill. Kendra never learned to play cards, but Jeff did, and he was glad to be invited to play again. He hadn't played a good game of spades since the Navy.

Jeff, who'd grown up in a much smaller family than Kendra, wasn't used to the chaos of a large family dinner, but he loved it. Everyone told him how much they loved the house.

"It's still a work in progress," he told them.

"But it's so big!" Uncle Rick responded. "This place is going to be a historical landmark when you're done. They'll be calling this The Gray House for hundreds of years."

Jeff didn't know how much Kendra's uncle really believed that, and how much of his statement was influenced by the number of Blue Moons he'd consumed. Several of their family members echoed the same sentiments, though. They loved the size of the house, they loved the location, they loved the improvements Jeff and Kendra made. For all of the troubles they'd had along the way, the family dinner confirmed what Jeff had suspected all along: this house was his triumph.

Fifteen - Status Update
December, 2011

The mayor's computer was still signed in; Jeff accessed the Internet easily. He signed in to his Facebook account. He went to the page for Channel 23, WWBT, the television station owned by the Willow Bend Tribune. He wrote on the station's wall, "Give me liberty or give me death."

Then he accessed his personal Facebook home page. Jeff typed in a new status: "Today I died. I died for the freedom of you and your children, so you may maintain your properties and live at peace, freely, in your personal castles. I ask your forgiveness for the people I harmed in the process. I am so sorry I brought shame on any of you. I pray you see me as a freedom fighter and understand my heart. I wish you all long lives. Goodbye. :~)"

He hit "Post."

It all seemed so final. Jeff wondered if he could still get out of city hall. Though ready to die, if it came to that, he didn't want to die. Escape seemed impossible, with police and fire fighters surrounding him, but he had to know if a way existed.

Jeff considered what would happen if he surrendered. Assuming the police didn't shoot him anyway before he had the chance, he could let himself get arrested, taken to jail, and tried. Some would sympathize with him in his war against the city. Over the course of this fight, he'd often contemplated whether it would be worth it to live behind bars, or whether death would be preferable. At least if he were in prison, Kendra would be spared the pain of his death. She'd still lose him, though. After he blew up the house and killed Erin Clarke's daughter, drove his car through city hall and beat Jonathon to death, he'd earned a harsh sentence. The state would consider him a domestic terrorist.

Jeff smirked as he logged out of his Facebook account. He'd never thought of himself as a terrorist. He'd been terrorized many times in his life; this was the first time he wasn't on the receiving end. He had to stick to his guns, literally and figuratively. He had to believe he was fighting for freedom. He had to believe what Princess City, and what he assumed thousands of other communities like it across America, were doing was wrong.

He thought again of Kendra and her family. Wade Wilson had a few more months before he retired from his long, exemplary career in public service as a police officer. Jeff wondered how Wade would react to the stigma of having a "home-grown terrorist" for a son-in-law...even though he believed Wade would agree with the reasoning behind his actions, if not the actions themselves. He hoped Wade would somehow be proud of him for standing up for all those weaker citizens who simply put up with the government's shit.

The rest of the family, he knew, would never forgive him. Jeff considered Lex dead to him already, but he'd earned Candace's respect over the course of his marriage to her only daughter. All that would be blown away when Candace found out what Jeff had done.

He ran his hands through his hair. Could he put the family through a trial? Could he really put himself through it: Lex, Erin Clarke, Justine Ernsberger, Earl McGhee, Katherine Tate and everyone else who had a complaint against him parading before a judge? Could he stand them talking about his aggressiveness, his tendency to be an asshole, how they believed all this time Jeff was a ticking time bomb waiting for an excuse to go off?

A flare of pain in Jeff's face reminded him the shotgun blast had hurt him. Without a mirror in the mayor's office, he couldn't see the extent of the damage. It hurt like hell, and though the bleeding seemed to have stopped, he felt weak from the loss of blood. He wondered how long he could go on like this before he'd need a trip to the ER.

He stood on the mayor's desk. He reached up, grasped a panel of the drop ceiling and pushed it up into the ceiling, out of his way. Sticking his head inside, he looked around in all directions, looking for a passageway, some way to get outside. He saw no way out.

Jeff took full responsibility for his actions. The consequence for the path he'd chosen was death. Jeff believed that the government by the people for the people was losing. Business had suckered the people by propping up puppet politicians. His death was going to be a bold statement that showed these puppets who was in charge.

Then he thought of the little girl who'd died. The thought he had ended a precious life sickened him. He threw up on the floor. The plumbing inspector and the mayor didn't bother him, but the thought of the little child, suffering in an explosion, horrified him. He let out a scream of disgust, as he spit the remaining bile from his mouth, wishing he could take back those actions.

The mayor's cell phone buzzed again. Jeff's heart ached at the thought Kendra might reverse-dial him. He didn't want to slip and say anything to upset or alarm her. Jeff had said his goodbye.

He picked up the phone, and a picture flashed across the display screen: Justine Ernsberger. Relieved, he answered the call. "Hello?"

"Jonathon?" Justine asked.

Jeff laughed. "Guess again. That bloated sack of shit is dead. I only wish you were here too."

"Who is this?" Justine asked, her voice rough with panic. "What's going on? What have you done?"

"Justine, you need to be more concerned about what you've done. You and the rest of you fascists at city hall, you petty tyrants who tried to lord it over me all these years, had this day of reckoning coming." He laughed again.

Justine went ballistic, cursing and screaming into the phone. That same second, the office phone rang. "Please hold," Jeff said over her. He set the cell phone down and let her continue her rant. He picked up the headset of the office phone.

"Hello?"

Captain Michael Fisher spoke on the other end. "Jeff, you've already gotten what you wanted, an interview with the media. Now let's end this."

"What are you talking about?" Jeff asked.

"There are TV crews all over out here. They're running your story on the local news. I'm not sure how you did it, but it's done. You got what you were after. Let's end this."

"Hold on," Jeff said. He went across the room and turned on the mayor's TV. He flipped through the channels until he reached Channel 23. The reporter on the screen stood in front of 149 North Cedar Street. From Jeff's house, the camera panned up the street, showing all the fire trucks and emergency vehicles around town hall.

"Minutes ago, Jeffrey Gray left a chilling message on WWBT's official Facebook wall," the reporter said. "It read, simply, 'Give me liberty or give me death. ' Gray is one of WWBT's Facebook friends, so we were able to access his public profile. These pictures show Jeff Gray and his wife, Kendra. WWBT has not been able to contact Kendra Gray at this time."

The camera panned back to the reporter. It was Sidney Broadbent, the one whose name the mayor kept in his private cell phone. Broadbent spoke with the owner of the florist shop, Blair Robins. "You know Jeff Gray?" the reporter asked her.

"He's my next door neighbor and has been for almost ten years," Blair said to the camera. "Jeff's a great guy. He shovels my walkway in the winter and sweeps away my leaves in the fall. I knew he'd been having issues with the city, but I never thought he'd do anything like this. He must've just snapped."

Blair's words opened the floodgates of Jeff's held-back emotions. He wept as he watched the screen. He'd truly had friends, people who believed in him. It hurt him to let them down like this, but he knew what he had to do.

Jeff also realized some would consider him the villain and Jonathon the hero. He stood over Jonathon, then delivered a vicious kick to the mayor's gut. Jonathon groaned. Jeff's eyes widened as he realized the mayor wasn't dead.

Jeff cracked a smile. Maybe his plans to make the mayor suffer were working out after all.

Behind him, he heard his own voice, distorted as it came from a mini-tape recorder, on Channel 23. The TV station was playing the interview he'd given with Broadbent. He paused to listen to himself:

"What I've done today will make them think twice before they ever do it to a citizen again. The revolution is coming; I'm just planting the seeds. Everyone may not see it this way, but I'm a freedom fighter. They've tried to steal my freedom, and I'm paying for it with my life. One day, people will see my death was for their freedom, like the patriots in the American Revolution. That's it; that's all I wanted to say."

Sixteen - Discoveries
May 2008

On a spring evening in 2008, Jeff and Kendra got a phone call from Lex. Jeff picked up the phone. "We're getting married!" Lex said.

"Congratulations," Jeff said. "You mean, you and Adrienne, right?"

"Of course."

"Are you drunk?"

Lex laughed. "Maybe a little bit."

"I'm just checking. Because when you told us Adrienne was pregnant with Rose, you swore you and Adrienne were never going to get married."

"Things change," Lex said. "I asked Adrienne to marry me, and she said yes. The girls are excited." Shortly after Lex moved in with Adrienne, she told him she was pregnant again. Once again, Lex claimed he'd been drunk. Their younger daughter's name was Delilah. "I want you to be one of my groomsmen, Jeff."

"Well, congratulations, and thank you. Here, I'll let you talk to your sister." He passed the phone to Kendra. She all but sat on Jeff's lap, trying to overhear the conversation. She pushed the speaker phone button and set the phone down.

"When are you getting married?" Kendra asked her brother.

"July sixteenth. We're getting married at the courthouse in LaPorte by a judge Monique works for." Like Candace Wilson, Monique was a legal clerk.

"Congratulations," Kendra said. "It's very exciting. Have you told Mom and Dad yet?"

"I wanted to, and I thought I had their mobile phone number, but I guess I don't," Lex said. Wade and Candace had gone to Florida on vacation that week, as they did for one week every spring.

"I'll get it for you," Kendra said. "You know Mom; she'll be mad if she isn't one of the first people to know." She gave him both Wade's and Candace's phone numbers, then added, "What made you change your mind?"

"It was time," Lex said. Jeff wondered what he meant. "Hey, I'll talk to you soon. I'm going to give Mom and Dad a call."

"Okay," she said. "Bye bye."

"That was interesting," Jeff said as he pushed "end."

"To say the least," she said. "I didn't see that one coming."

The weekend before the wedding, the best man, Lex's friend (and fry cook) Jim, was supposed to throw a bachelor party for Lex, complete with a stripper and a live band. Jim's plan never came to fruition, though, and instead he gave Lex the two hundred dollars he had planned to pay the stripper and suggested they all cross the state line to the Pokagon Potawatomi Indian casino in Michigan.

The casino's décor reflected its Native American ownership. It looked like an enormous pine lodge. Right off the bat, Jeff won six hundreds dollars. Kendra took her Malibu rum and pineapple juice and sat down at the slot machine Jeff had gotten lucky on, but she lost the twenty dollars in cash she'd had on her. Jeff sat at the machine next to her and won another two hundred dollars.

"A round of drinks for all of us!" Jeff yelled out.

Kendra's forehead crinkled up and her eyes narrowed. Jeff could tell she was upset about him spending money on drinks. They were barely getting by and they needed those winnings. "Uncrinkle that forehead," Jeff growled into Kendra's ear. "I just won eight hundred dollars and we're going to have some fun." As if Jeff had flipped a switch, Kendra's face washed with calm. She smiled and gave him a kiss.

Lex and Adrienne were ready to leave around two in the morning. Jeff had sobered up enough to drive them and some friends to Lex and Adrienne's. Jeff and Kendra decided not to stay.

"Are you sure you want to go?" Jim asked them. "I was going to get a bonfire going in the back yard and fire off a few rounds into the corn field." He showed Jeff and Kendra the gun in his coat pocket.

"No thanks," Jeff said. When he was a kid, a friend shot Jeff in the eyebrow with a pellet gun. He still had the scar. Jeff was nervous around strangers with guns. He also couldn't get it out of his head that Lex had said years earlier how someone could disappear out there in the corn fields. He drove Kendra home, where they went straight to bed.

On the day of the wedding, a secretary guided Jeff, Kendra and Lex to the small courtroom where the ceremony would take place. "Adrienne wanted the big courtroom on the third floor," Lex explained. "It has these great stained glass windows; you probably saw them from outside. But one of the other judges is in the middle of a murder trial, so this is the best they could do. Our judge is squeezing us in between two other weddings."

Wade arrived next. Candace was supposed to be following him, with Adrienne's mother Eileen in her car. Monique would drive her sister and the three kids. In theory, they would all arrive shortly after Wade, but in practice, the group waited twenty more minutes before Kendra looked out the window and spied Eileen on the corner across the street. "Here they come," she told everyone.

"Remember," Wade told his son, "when the judge gets here, plead not guilty." Everyone laughed.

"I'd plead insanity if I were him," Jeff added.

Candace arrived in the lavender suit Kendra had helped her pick out. Eileen, who wore red, and Monique, whose dress was white with red trim, followed. Kendra almost matched, in a white summer dress with black and purple roses. Rose and Delilah looked like princesses in their full-skirted pink gowns and red, glittering slippers.

When Adrienne entered the room, she looked amazing. She'd had her hair, back to its natural dark blonde color, done up in curls and a tiara. She wore a diamond solitaire necklace. Her white dress was similar to her daughters', with short sleeves and full skirt. She carried a bouquet of white roses and baby's breath.

The judge arrived another twenty minutes after the bride. "Let's make a half-circle in front of the bench," the judge said. When the short ceremony ended, Jeff and Kendra hugged Adrienne and Lex. The wedding party exited, past a line of reporters and tight security due to the murder trial, and walked onto the front lawn of the courthouse, where the wedding photographer had set up. After posing for a few pictures, Jeff and Kendra got back in their car and headed for the reception, at McNamara's Irish Pub.

During a slow song, Jeff danced with Adrienne while Kendra danced with Lex. "It's about fucking time he married you," Jeff told Adrienne.

"I know," Adrienne said, smiling.

"You'll find out it's like pulling teeth trying to get Lex or Kendra to take responsibility sometimes. It's hard to understand; I don't know what makes them so afraid."

Adrienne said, "I know; I don't understand it either." They finished their dance, and Jeff danced with Kendra.

The wedding reception lasted until the pub closed down. Eileen and her husband Kirk left to take the kids to a baby-sitter before coming back, and Adrienne's grandparents went home by nine, but by and large the adults stayed to close the place down. They all had a blast.

*****

One Sunday in November, Kendra sat on the living room carpet, the newspaper spread out in front of her. The Grays' fat, brown striped cat Applesauce spread herself out on the stack of ads Kendra had set off to the left. To her right, Kendra kept a cup of coffee and a small pile of mini chocolate bars. She gradually worked her way through the coffee and chocolate as she read her paper. Jeff sat on the couch, flipping between the Sunday public affairs programs on TV.

"Hey," Kendra said, "the town's having a meeting on Tuesday night to talk about their plans for expanding the River Walk. We should go."

"Absolutely," Jeff said.

Alfred Stewart Park had opened the previous fall. Jeff and Kendra loved to walk across it. Mallard ducks and Canada geese graced the shallow waters, and the island had a large, grassy lawn in the middle.

Where the waterway returned to the natural river, construction workers prepared to make a bridge across to Battell Park. A new sidewalk already connected Stewart Park to the natural island a few paces west of it.

Many years before, one of the town's main industries was a brewery operated by the O'Laughlin family. They used the shallow channel between the island and the shore to turn their mill wheel. The O'Laughlins built the brewery on the shore, with a foot bridge running out to the island. For years they used the island as a garbage dump, abandoning outdated machines there as they purchased newer technology. When the brewery shut down, a beer museum in Wisconsin bought many of the abandoned machines. The city bought the island at the same time they bought the land for Stewart Park. Stewart Park stood on what had been the rubber plant, which had gone out of business in the early 1990s. In 2000, the town imploded the abandoned rubber factory amid much pomp and ceremony.

Where the rubber plant's parking lots and smoke stack had once stood, the town had contracted a steel company to build condos. A line of condos now overlooked O'Laughlin Island, though demand wasn't as great as the developers predicted. It took a long time before the first one sold, and the developer struggled to make any new sales. Some people called them an eyesore. A new block of condos also stood on the north side of the river, looking across the water to Stewart Park.

All of these changes fascinated Jeff, who enjoyed the progress the town had already made around the river, and thought the additional changes could only increase his property value.

"What time is that meeting?" he asked Kendra.

"Six-thirty," she said. "Damn it, I'll still be at work, unless I leave early."

"Don't worry about it," Jeff said. "I'll go, and I'll tell you what the town's plans are when you get home. This is kind of exciting."

"Yeah," she said, as Applesauce got up from the ads, stretched, and plopped herself down on the page Kendra was about to turn. "I'll save the article so we don't forget…if I can ever get the cat off it."

As he worked Monday and Tuesday, Jeff couldn't help but look forward to the meeting Tuesday night. When he finished working for the day, he came home, showered, shaved, and got dressed in casual clothes. On this chilly fall night, Jeff walked to town hall and found the meeting room. Jeff arrived a half hour early, the first to arrive.

At the front of the meeting room, a woman in her early forties with light brown hair, dressed in a long, heather-gray skirt, a white blouse, and gray leather boots stood holding a clipboard. Beside her, a detailed map of the north and south banks of the river, covered in dots and Xs, stood on an easel.

"Hi, Jeff. How are you?" the woman said.

Jeff remembered her: Erin Clarke, the city planner. He'd had to come to her office and talk to her when he'd torn the old, moldy porch off the side of his house and replaced it with a new, attached mud room. The town planner had to make sure he stayed within the boundaries of his property line.

"I'm doing fine," he replied to her. "How about you?"

"I'm doing well," she said.

Jeff took a seat in the front row. Moments later, two men entered and sat behind Jeff. One of them, a well-groomed fifty-something gentleman in a soft gray business suit, Jeff recognized as John Harrison, the owner of the Wellington mansion and operator of its bed and breakfast. To his right, in a neatly tucked flannel shirt and designer jeans, sat John's partner, Quinn Jordan. John owned the first house on Edgewater Drive, the one directly across from the florist shop;

he used it as a rental property. Jeff had seen him raking leaves or shoveling snow at his rental property. None of his tenants seemed to stay very long, and at the moment, the house sat vacant. Jeff and Kendra met John and Quinn one night when, while out on their walk, they stopped into the Wellington Mansion for a drink.

After that night, Jeff and Kendra waved whenever they saw John working on the rental house, and when they saw John and Quinn eating at Cloverfield's East. John didn't seem to recognize them, though. He never returned their friendly gestures. Jeff came to believe John looked down on him because the outside of the house was still ugly.

He got that same uneasy feeling as he sat next to John at the meeting. The room began to fill. Jeff saw the Montoyas and several of his other neighbors from Edgewater Drive. Soon, Erin called the meeting to order.

"Good evening," she said. "For those of you who haven't met me, my name is Erin Clarke, and I'm the town planner. I'm sure all of you are familiar with the River Walk, which extends from Logan Street in the west to O'Laughlin Island and Alfred Stewart Park along the south bank of the river, then across the river to Central Park in the east, through Battell Park and back to Logan Street."

She went over all the improvements the town had done. Her PowerPoint presentation showed maps, photos and drawings of the improvements at Central Park, continuing all the way to the opening of Stewart Park. She mentioned how the citizens in the condos on the west side of the old O'Laughlin Brewery had sued the city for losing their view.

"They originally won their law suit against the city, saying the new pedestrian bridge ruined their view of the river and devalued their homes," Erin explained."But then, one of the condo owners sold his home for a greater value than what it had appraised for ten years before. The city appealed the verdict in the law suit, and the city prevailed."

She droned on for forty-five minutes, talking about all the different stages of the River Walk. "All of these changes have improved the property values around the area," Erin said. "Our next plan is to go down Edgewater Drive as we repair the Princess Avenue Bridge. Ultimately, we'll expand the River Walk to include Silver Park. We're going to build a walkway along the north bank of the river."

The citizens muttered. A woman stood and asked, "How can you do that when we have boathouses down there? That's our private property."

"I don't want strangers walking on my lawn; I don't care if it is separated from my house by the road. People will get into our boathouses and vandalize our stuff."

"Yeah," someone else added. "What will it do to our insurance rates?"

"Why not make the end of Edgewater a cul-de-sac and improve the sidewalk we already have?" someone else suggested.

"Look," Erin said, "we can do this with or without your permission. The city has egress rights ten feet from the edge of the road, so legally, we have the right to do this. We're just trying to get your opinions on how to do this as a courtesy."

"You can't do this," one of Jeff's neighbors shouted. "We'll vote you out of office!"

"Even if you vote us out, this is still going to happen," Erin said. "The city council is on board with this; this is what the city council wants."

"Then we'll vote them out, too," someone shouted. "Don't you people understand the meaning of the words 'private property?'"

Mayor Jonathon, who sat off to the side throughout Erin's presentation, stood and said, "I'll take responsibility for this. Let me assure you, this is going to happen. If you want to blame anybody, blame me."

A thousand things ran through Jeff's mind; he felt he had to say something. Jeff said, "The only time we've ever had any crime around our neighborhood is during the summer festival. This is going to make access to the festival easier, but it's going to create more crimes."

"Exactly what I was thinking," someone in the crowd agreed. "I had my garage broken into this past summer. The festival ends at nine or ten, and then these teenagers hang around for a few more hours with nothing better to do than cause trouble."

After more discussion, Erin called the meeting to an end. As angry citizens filed out, Jeff got up to study the maps on the easels. When he found his house on the map, Jeff noticed the red, dotted line along the river side of Edgewater Drive crossed Cedar Street and continued to follow the river bank.

He asked Erin, "Why are there red dots going by my house? How do you expect to put a River Walk in there when my house is fifteen feet off the river bank?"

Erin told him, "Jeff, it's going through your house."

Jeff said, "What does that mean? You're going to tear down my house to build a sidewalk?"

Erin nodded.

"So you're telling me if I do any more improvements to my home, if I put one more nail into my house, I'm feeding a dead horse?"

Erin nodded again.

"Okay, fine," Jeff sighed. "You give me one of those condos over by O'Laughlin Island and you can have my house."

"We'll see what we can do for you," she said.

"Well, what's the process?"

"We have to get two appraisals on your house, we'll offer you the average of the two and then we'll issue a condemnation order."

"Let's get this over with then; I don't want to waste any more time on a house I'm going to lose. Call me tomorrow." He gave Erin his number.

When he got home, Jeff told Kendra what he learned from the meeting. She reacted with shock, then anger.

"I was pissed off at first, too," Jeff said. "Then I thought about it, and this might be the best thing that ever happened to us."

"Being homeless?" Kendra asked.

Jeff chuckled. "They can't take our property without compensating us for it, and I'm pretty sure the law says they have to give us enough to relocate."

"It would be nice if we could find another place near here," Kendra answered. "I do love this neighborhood. We never intended to leave it."

"Once the town pays off our mortgage, we could go anywhere, really. We could start out with an inexpensive, but finished, house in a great location. We'd have a clean slate, all of our debts paid off."

"We need that," Kendra said. "It's starting to be your slow season again, and they keep talking on the news about how bad the economy is getting. I hope when the new president gets sworn in, the economy will rebound, but that's still going to be a couple more months. In the meantime, it's getting hard to come up with the money for our bills."

"I know," Jeff said. "Wouldn't it be nice to have our house paid for? We could live anywhere. We could go to Iowa or Nebraska and get a little cabin out in the middle of nowhere. We'd never have to worry about local government bureaucratic bullshit again."

"Then we should move to Key West," Kendra said. "It's warm, and the local government is probably pretty lax and mellow."

"I've heard just the opposite. The citizens are laissez-faire, but the town government's very protective and hands-on."

"Oh," she said. "Not our kind of place, then."

"I do like the idea of living somewhere warm, though," Jeff said. "We could live in Hawaii. I was reading online the other day about these really cheap, ramshackle houses they have out there. Living expenses are high, but it's not hard to get a house in Hawaii."

"I would love that," Kendra said. "Tropical weather all year long, privacy, not very many neighbors, an amazing local culture..."

"Volcanoes," Jeff added. "Scorpions, too. It's also far away; you wouldn't see your family much anymore."

"I would miss them, especially my mom and dad," she said. "I guess we'd get a webcam and see them online all the time. It might be worth it to live in Hawaii."

That night, Jeff researched local river front property values. What he found out encouraged him. He knew for sure he and Kendra had already turned their $67,500 house into a $250,000 house, and with the prices the new condos went for, he expected his house was worth more than ever.

Two appraisers came out the following week. Jeff prepared. He and Kendra made a list of all the amenities their house offered - the whirlpool tub, direct access to the water and water rights, the vaulted ceilings on the second floor - and everything they'd planned to do with it in the future. At one time, Jeff had made elaborate plans to build a garage onto the front of the house, mimicking the structure of the house itself. He still had detailed drawings of his design, and he included these in the packet he handed to the appraiser.

He also included the specifications of the condos to the east of O'Laughlin Island. Some of them were nearly identical to Jeff and Kendra's house in square footage, though the builder considered them two-bedroom homes, and Jeff and Kendra's had four. They both believed it would be a very fair trade.

Jeff and Kendra had had an appraisal on their home a few years earlier, when they wanted to refinance and get rid of some of Kendra's student loans and credit cards they'd foolishly maxed out. That appraisal was for $178,000, and Jeff considered it an insult. The appraiser had only compared their home to waterfront properties in Willow Bend; Princess City had a better school system and a much lower crime rate. He and Kendra continued to make repairs in the meantime, and he knew the appraisal would come back for no less than $250,000 this time. Jeff and Kendra were excited about their possibilities. They expected an offer of $300,000 or more.

The first appraiser accepted the thick packet of materials Jeff had copied for him, saying, "I'll take these into consideration." Jeff handed the same packet to the second appraiser.

When the appraisers finished, Jeff called Erin Clarke's office and asked Erin when he and Kendra could expect to have the town make an offer on their home. "We're really anxious to get this over with," he said. "Like I told you at the meeting, I don't want to keep feeding a dead horse."

"You'll have an offer by Christmas," Erin told him. There was nothing more for Jeff and Kendra to do but wait.

Seventeen - Insults and Injuries
November, 2008

In the middle of November, Jeff and Kendra got invited to Isaac's wedding. Lex's best friend was marrying Lily Bowerman, daughter of a former Cloverfield's manager. The one time they'd met Lily, at one of Lex and Adrienne's bonfires, she seemed like a sweet person, someone good for Isaac. Jeff had remarked, "Lily acts like someone who doesn't like to take shit off anybody. I hope Isaac can deal with that." Coming from Jeff, that was a compliment.

The day of Lily and Isaac's ceremony, it rained. In fact, as soon as Jeff and Kendra stepped out of their new Toyota Matrix, the rain poured down on them. They waved hello to Lily's parents Marcus and Tina in the front row, then sat directly behind Wade, Candace, and Adrienne. Lex stood in as one of the groomsman, and the Wilsons sat in for Isaac's parents. Isaac's father had died in a commuter train accident when Isaac was a teen, and his mother had recently died from complications of asthma. Isaac was always welcomed into the Wilson's home. He was like another son to them.

The rain stopped during the ceremony, and by the time Jeff and Kendra reached the reception hall, the night had warmed up. The reception had a Polish-style buffet and an open bar. Jeff stuck to beer, and Kendra drank white wine.

After dinner and dancing, she switched to lemon-lime soda. Jeff stopped drinking beer when Lily's mom cut the wedding cake.

As they sat at the table, eating their wedding cake, Monique came and sat by Jeff and Kendra. "Hey, guys," she said. "I haven't seen you since my sister's wedding. How are you?"

"We're okay," Jeff said. "We did just find out the city's going to take our house."

"No way!" Monique said. "I love your house; it's so big and beautiful. Did they tell you what they're taking it for?"

"To turn it into a sidewalk," Kendra answered. "They want to expand the River Walk all the way to Silver Park, and our house is in the way."

"But at least they're going to pay you for it, right?" Monique asked.

"We're waiting for them to give us an offer," Jeff said. "They sent two appraisers last week."

"Well, good luck," Monique said. "I hope they give you a lot for it." They thanked her.

Jeff and Kendra had a good time, staying long after Candace and Wade went home. They stayed until the reception ended and helped the Bowermans clean up. They finished stacking chairs for the Bowermans when Lex, three sheets to the wind, came up to them and said, "The bartender says we only finished off two-thirds of the keg. Come to the bar with me and help me drain it."

"I could maybe have one more beer," Jeff said. Hours after he'd had his last drink, he felt sober. "Adrienne is looking for you, though. She's ready to go home." Adrienne was also sober, having drunk coffee all night.

Adrienne came up to them. "Come on, Lex," she said. "I just talked to the baby-sitter, and she said Rose is sick. She's throwing up."

"No, she's not," Lex replied. "I guarantee you Rose is not sick."

Jeff was surprised by Lex being so emphatic that Adrienne was wrong. He remembered that Lex had told him years before that Adrienne tells "white lies" all of the time and he attributed it to that.

Adrienne shrugged. "We should still get home."

"You go home with the girls," Lex said. "I'll drive myself home after Isaac and I drain the keg."

"Okay," Adrienne said in a tone that indicated the opposite. "We'll talk about it in the morning."

"We'll make sure he gets home safely," Jeff promised her.

"Thanks, you guys," Adrienne said. "I'll see you some other time."

"Yeah," Kendra said. "At Thanksgiving, if not before then."

Jeff and Kendra stuck close by Lex for the next hour, following him to the bar and then outside, where he smoked a cigarette. When he got done smoking, he said, "I'm going to go home now."

"I'll drive you," Jeff said. "Kendra, are you sober?"

"I'm fine," she said. "I've been drinking soda for the past few hours."

"I'm fine, too. Lex, you come with me in my car, and Kendra will follow behind us in your car."

"I need my car," Lex said. "I have to do inventory at work tomorrow."

Kendra laughed. "You're not listening, Lex," she said. "He said I'd take your car home for you. You and your car will both end up your house, and then Jeff will take me home in our own car."

"Give me your keys," Jeff said, holding out his hand to Lex.

Lex shook his head. "I can drive myself in my own car. I don't want anybody else driving my car."

"Lex, you're drunk," Jeff said. "You drive and you'll probably kill yourself, or somebody else. Don't make me ask you again; give me your keys."

"No," Lex said. "Jeff, I can drive drunk better than any of you can."

"But you can't drive drunk," Kendra told him. "That's not okay, and we're not going to enable you. Give Jeff your keys. If you don't want to give Jeff your keys, then give me your keys."

"No," Lex insisted. "I'm the best fucking drunk driver you've ever seen." He got loud and obnoxious, and people started to gather around and tell him to give up his keys.

When he took his keys out of his pocket, though, Jeff took them from his hand. Lex grabbed for them, but Jeff stuck them in his inside jacket pocket.

"Give me my keys, damn it!" Lex yelled at Jeff. "Don't make me fight you."

Jeff snickered; he looked twice Lex's size. "Stop being an asshole, you drunk asshole," Jeff said. "You're drunk, and you're not getting your keys back. Kendra and I will drive you home. We'll take your car if you want. I'll drive, you get in the passenger seat, and Kendra will follow us in my car."

Lex didn't listen. "Give me my keys!"

"No!" Jeff said.

Lex started to take off his jacket. "Okay, I'll fight you for them."

Before he could finish taking his jacket off, Jeff came up behind him and got Lex in a bear hug.

"Stop it," Jeff told him. "Just stop it!"

"Let me go!" Lex screamed, struggling against Jeff. He tried several times to head-butt Jeff. "Let me go, god damn it!" Jeff saw it coming each time and moved his head out of the way.

"Lex, what's the matter with you?" Kendra shouted. "Calm down. Stop trying to hit Jeff with your head!"

By then, Isaac and Marcus had come out to see the commotion in the parking lot. "What's going on?" Marcus asked Kendra. She told him.

Isaac got in Lex's face. "Lex, calm down, man. Jeff, he's going to calm down. You're going to calm down, aren't you, Lex?"

"I'll calm down when he gives me my fucking keys!" Lex hollered. He'd stopped trying to head-butt Jeff, but Jeff still had him in a bear hug.

"Jeff, let him go," Marcus said. "He's going to calm down now. Lex, are you listening to me? This is my daughter's wedding, and I'm responsible for all the guests getting home safely. If anything happens to you, everyone will blame me, and I can't have that. Let your brother-in-law drive you home."

"I need my car!" Lex yelled. "I've got to do inventory tomorrow."

"Jeff will drive you home in your car," Kendra told him again. "I'll follow him. We'll all get home, and everyone will be in their own vehicle."

"Do what they're telling you, Lex," Marcus pleaded. "You'll be able to do your inventory and everything will be fine. Don't make this a bigger scene than it needs to be. Jeff, let him go."

Jeff let go of Lex, who spun around to face him. "This is why everybody in the family hates you!" Lex screamed at Jeff. "You're nothing but a self-righteous, arrogant asshole. You're not happy unless everybody does what you say." He turned to his sister. "How can you put up with him? You do whatever he says, like you're some damn puppet with his hand up your ass!"

Kendra looked horrified. Jeff put his arm around her. He raged inside, almost ready to tell Lex to drive himself home and kill himself. He knew he couldn't do that to Wade and Candace, though, or to some innocent person who might get in Lex's way. Jeff knew he was damned either way.

"Give me my fucking keys!" Lex shouted again and again.

"I'm sorry for the scene he's making," Jeff told Isaac and Marcus. "I'm sorry he's doing this on your day. I'm not going to give him these keys, though. He's way too wasted to drive."

"I'm with you," Marcus said. "Why don't you give me his keys? I'll hold on to them; you call his wife and see if she can come pick him up."

Jeff said, "No, I'll keep his keys."

He locked himself and Kendra in his own car to get enough peace and quiet to call Adrienne while Lex hammered on the windows and continued to scream, "You're not my father! You can't tell me what to do! Give me my fucking keys!"

"Hello?" Adrienne answered the phone, sounding as if she'd been sleeping.

"Adrienne, I'm sorry to bother you," Jeff said. "Lex is drunk, and he's trying to drive himself home, so I took his keys. He's out here telling me how the whole family hates me and trying to fight me, but I'm not giving him his keys back. Can you get your sister to keep an eye on the girls while you pick him up?"

"Yeah," Adrienne said. "I'll be there in a little bit." The reception hall was twenty minutes from Monique's house, so Jeff knew he would be waiting a while. All he cared about was making sure Lex got home, though after Lex had been so vicious, he wasn't sure why he cared.

As Jeff and Kendra waited in the car, and Marcus seemed to have gotten Lex calmed down and got him back inside the reception hall, Jeff turned to Kendra and said, "I told your brother if he ever disrespected me like this again, I wouldn't have anything else to do with him."

"I know," she said. "I can't believe how upset he is with me. What did we do to him, try to make sure he was safe? The nerve of us! I know he's really drunk, but I never realized what a mean drunk he is!"

"Remember the bonfire when he got totally wasted and wouldn't stop talking about what a shit country the United States is, and how he'd rather live in any other country?" Jeff said. "He's a vicious drunk. He's a vicious person who gives the impression of being the nicest guy in the world. I'm tired of waiting. We're going home."

"We still have Lex's keys," Kendra pointed out.

"Fuck him," Jeff replied. "He can come get them tomorrow morning."

The next morning, Jeff and Kendra waited for Lex's phone call. Eventually, it came. "I'm sorry," Lex said. "I need to get my keys from you, though. I have to be at work at noon; I'll be there at quarter 'til to pick up my keys."

"Okay," Kendra said. "Lex, when you get here, you'd damn well better apologize for what you said and did last night. Do you even remember what you did?"

"Yeah," Lex said. "We'll talk about it when I get there." He hung up.

Kendra went upstairs, where Jeff filled the whirlpool tub for a soak. She relayed to him what Lex had said.

"You can talk to him," Jeff told her. "I'm so pissed at that fucker right now, I don't even want to look at him. The very fact that he's not going to be here until fifteen minutes before he has to work means any apology he tries to make isn't going to be sincere. If he sincerely wanted to apologize to me, he would sit down with me and spend enough time with me to make me understand why he acted like he did. That can't be done in fifteen minutes."

"You're right," Kendra said.

"I don't know if I'll ever have anything to do with your brother again," Jeff said. "He broke my heart last night. How dare he speak for the whole family and say they hate me?"

"My family doesn't hate you," Kendra said, putting her arms around Jeff. "They love you. What Lex said was drunk talk; he was irrationally angry. He told me I was a puppet with your hand up my ass; I should be as pissed at him as you are."

"You're right," he said. "I can't even look at the stupid fucker, though. You deal with him."

As Kendra explained to Jeff later, Lex apologized in the insincere and hasty way Jeff anticipated. He took his keys and kept repeating he had to go to work. He made it clear to Kendra he couldn't have cared less about her feelings or Jeff's.

"Jeff says you need to make an appointment and set aside some time to make an apology to him," Kendra told Lex.

Lex never did. That Monday morning, Jeff went to Wade's house while Candace and Kendra were both at work and had a heart-to-heart talk with his father-in-law. Jeff confessed he may have been wrong for some of the things he said and did to Lex, but it broke his heart that Lex couldn't bring himself to make a proper apology to him. He told Wade about his fear the family really did hate him.

"I'm tired of them making me out to be the asshole all the time," Jeff said, breaking down in tears. "I'm so sick of it!"

"We don't hate you," Wade said. "You're Kendra's husband!" Wade stood up and said, "Come here, come here." As Jeff stood up, bawling, Wade gave him a hug, something Wade didn't do, and told him not to listen to Lex's drunken ramblings. Wade made Jeff feel a little better, but the night of Isaac's wedding continued to haunt Jeff's thoughts like a bad dream.

Jeff got angrier and angrier as days passed, and still no apologetic phone call came from Lex. A week later, on Thanksgiving, Jeff felt broken-hearted. Every one of the eight years he and Kendra had been together, they'd had a Thanksgiving meal with the Wilsons. This year a peaceful Thanksgiving dinner seemed impossible.

"Why won't you go?" Kendra asked him that morning. "Why should you be the one to suffer? You didn't do anything wrong."

"You know that, and I know that, but your family still blames me," Jeff said. "I told you years ago, when I had to kick Lex out of the house, your mother would take Lex's side, no matter how stupid or unreasonable he's being. Has she called to tell me Lex was wrong, and that the family doesn't really hate me? Has she done anything to reassure me she loves me, to tell me I did the right thing when I stopped her son from driving drunk? No. She hasn't said a word to me. I don't expect her to get involved in it, but I do expect her to show she still cares about us."

"You can't blame my mother for this," Kendra said. "This doesn't have anything to do with her."

"She's made it have something to do with her," Jeff countered. "By now, she's listened to Lex's bullshit, his lies about me. She's listened to his skewed take on what happened that night, but she hasn't bothered to listen to us. If she cared about us, why wouldn't she at least listen to our side of the story? Why wouldn't she, at the very least, call you and try to get your side of the story?"

"I tried to talk to her," Kendra said. "She told me it was between me and my brother and she didn't want to get in the middle of it."

"And that's acceptable in your family," Jeff said angrily. "If someone doesn't want to talk about something, well, why would we make that person talk? Hide, stick your heads in the sand, and maybe if you ignore something long enough it will go away. I don't know what makes you guys so afraid of reality, but I wasn't raised that way. I was raised to take responsibility, and you treat me like I'm some kind of oddball because I expect other people to do the same."

"I don't think you're some kind of oddball at all," Kendra said. "Your way is better. My family's way of doing things is screwed up. I must say though, my family is mostly still together and everyone in your family is isolated, hating each other."

Several years before, when she and Jeff got into a lot of arguments, Kendra had to confess she had problems relating to people and taking responsibility for things. Her grandmother had serious addiction issues, and Kendra believed some family dysfunction was passed down through her mother. Even though Candace wasn't an alcoholic or a drug addict, she was trained to be an enabler.

Jeff, a church counselor in his young adulthood, wanted to help, but he didn't know what he should do. "I wish there was a way I could teach you about being set free, like they do in Christianity, without us having to go to church and be involved in a religion. We need a program, like AA or NA, that would teach you the 12-Step Program. That would help you understand," he had said.

"There is a 12-Step Program for family members of addicts," Kendra had said. "It's called Al-Anon."

For a year Kendra went twice a week, though she eventually stopped going.

"Whatever excuse you have for it, I'm not going to put up with it," Jeff said. "I can't even look at your brother without wanting to punch him in the face. Do you know he told me one time he's never been in a fight? At first I didn't believe him, because he's so into superheroes and kung-fu movies, and he's worked in bars, but he's never had to throw a punch in his life."

"I've never been in a fight, either," Kendra said. "I kind of think that's a good thing."

"But it isn't," Jeff explained. "Once you learn how to take a punch, get your bearings, fight back and get the other person to back down, you get the sense of being able to handle anything. You and Lex never had that, so all you know how to do is back down from a challenge and run away from it like cowards."

"Lex was going to fight you in the parking lot."

"Only because he was drunk," Jeff said. "He had artificial courage that night. Sometimes, though, I think I ought to beat his ass just so he could learn how to take it. You know I would never lay a hand on you; I'd expect you to leave me the first time I did. It's different with your brother, though."

"So come to Thanksgiving dinner and kick his ass," Kendra said. "Get it over with."

"No," Jeff said. "I'm not going to do it on Wade's property. Your dad's the one member of your family, other than you, I still have some respect for. He's the only one who's shown me any understanding."

"Do you think I should stay home with you?" Kendra asked him.

"That's entirely up to you," Jeff replied. "One thing I will never do is hurt you physically; the other thing I will never do is come between you and your family. If you want to see your mom and dad and your nieces, then go ahead. I understand, and I don't hold it against you at all. I want you to understand why I can't go, though."

Kendra decided to go to her parents' house for Thanksgiving. She kissed Jeff and told him she'd bring him back a Thanksgiving meal. Jeff kissed her too, sat down on the couch, turned on a movie, and took a nap.

When he woke up, Kendra was back with a plate of leftovers for him. "You won't believe what my mom said to me," Kendra told him. "First she tells me she doesn't want to get involved in what happened between Lex and us, but then she says, 'I don't care who apologizes to whom, as long as this whole thing is over by Christmas. ' As if you and I have anything to apologize about!"

Jeff shook his head. "If I did something wrong, I'll admit it. I won't be a coward about it like your brother. I can't think of anything I did wrong, though, when I tried to stop that fool from getting himself killed. I told you your mom would stick up for him, didn't I?"

"Yeah," Kendra said. "You were right. My brother cared more about his stupid restaurant inventory than he did about our feelings, and all she can do is take his side."

"This is all too depressing," Jeff said. "After I finish eating this, let's get bundled up and go for a walk."

Kendra agreed. The temperature held at a chilly thirty-four degrees, but it hadn't snowed yet, so they put on their winter gear and went for a walk along the River Walk.

"I don't know who I should be more upset about," Jeff said as he and Kendra walked across O'Laughlin Island. "Your brother, your mother, or the city."

"This has been a rough year for us," Kendra said. "Especially for you."

"I wonder if any of the bars are open," Jeff said. He needed a distraction from this miserable winter. They went through the downtown area and found an open bar near the railroad tracks. Jeff ordered a beer, and Kendra ordered a cranberry-flavored, bottled lemonade drink.

"Should we do a shot?" Jeff asked her.

"Why not?" Kendra said.

"You pick."

"Wild Turkey," she said. "It is Thanksgiving, after all." The bartender gave them their shots. Jeff and Kendra swallowed their whiskey.

"Whew!" Jeff muttered, "That's like fire."

Kendra coughed a little and said, "It sure isn't Jack."

They took the change from their drinks and put a dollar in the pool table. They played one game of pool, at which Jeff beat Kendra, then had a shot of tequila and a game of darts before they walked home.

"Until now, I thought this was going to be the worst Thanksgiving ever," Jeff told Kendra as they walked through the door.

Meanwhile, the stress of waiting for the city to give them an offer on their home made Jeff feel worse. Jeff and Kendra waited and waited, expecting the phone call every day. Jeff walked around the house saying, "When are we going to get that offer?"

"You have to be patient," Kendra kept telling him. "She'll probably call us tomorrow."

But Christmas Eve came and went without an offer. At one time, Christmas Eve meant a huge get-together with Candace's side of the family. This year no one in the family felt very much in the holiday spirit. The worsening economic news and rising unemployment made everyone scared to spend any money. Jeff's business had slowed down. The family decided to celebrate the holiday separately.

On Christmas Day, Candace called Kendra and asked her to come over for lunch. "Your brother and Adrienne won't be here," she said. "They're having Christmas at Adrienne's grandmother's house."

When she got off the phone with her mother, Kendra asked Jeff, "Will you come to Christmas with my mom and dad?"

"I'm still mad at your mother," Jeff told her. "I guess she and I will talk about it when we get there." Kendra had bought and wrapped presents for her parents, for her nieces, and for Adrienne, but nothing for Lex.

As Jeff walked through the door, Candace gave him a big hug. "I missed you at Thanksgiving," she said.

"I missed you, too," Jeff said. "I'm still upset with you, though."

"You're upset with me?" Candace said, stunned and indignant. "I didn't do anything to you! I don't want to talk about it any more. Can't we just get through one day without any of this shit?"

"But Lex told me the whole family hates me, and I never got a call from you or heard a word from you saying you didn't," Jeff said. He wiped the snow off his shoes, walked around her, and grabbed a bottle of beer from the refrigerator. "Jeff, I know you guys were right to take away Lex's keys. I never defended him for trying to drive drunk."

"You never defended me when Lex said the whole family hated me, either," Jeff said. "I can hardly figure you out, Candace. Sometimes you act so loving towards me, and at other times, I think you can hardly stand me."

"I do love you," Candace said. "I love my daughter, my son, my son-in-law, and my daughter-in-law, and because I have to love all of you, I can't take sides."

"That's sure not what it feels like," Jeff said.

By now, Wade had come up from his favorite chair in front of the TV in the basement. "We're not talking about this again, are we?" he asked.

"No," Jeff said. "We were done. I already said all I was going to say."

"Good, because that's going to give me a headache," Wade said. "Now let's eat." They had a nice meal, opened their presents, and it almost seemed like old times again. Jeff and Kendra talked excitedly about what they would do when the city bought their home.

For the rest of the day, Jeff couldn't stop thinking about the damage Lex had done. He called Lex's house, knowing full well Lex wouldn't have the balls to pick up the phone if he was home, or even to return Jeff's call. He was too much of a coward. Jeff needed to vent, though, so he called and left a message. "You know, Lex, you're the one who's so into superheroes. What do you want to be in this family, Lex? The hero, or the villain? Right now you've got this family so screwed up we can't even have dinners together. How long is it going to take before you'll fix this?"

Christmas came and went, and the city still hadn't made Jeff and Kendra an offer on their home.

Because he couldn't get it out of his head, Jeff spent many evenings researching further into property values in the neighborhood, until he felt like an expert. His hopes were high; he felt he and Kendra might be justified in asking for as much as $400,000 for their property.

"What's the absolute least amount of money we'll take for this house?" Jeff asked Kendra. "Three hundred and fifty thousand?"

"I think three hundred and fifty is fair," she said.

Three weeks after Christmas Jeff got a call from Erin Clarke. This was the moment he'd been waiting for.

"Jeff, we finally have the paperwork in. When can I set up a meeting with you?" Erin said.

"Can't you tell me over the phone?" Jeff asked.

"No, I typically meet with the homeowner in person." Erin said.

"I can come over there right now," Jeff said.

"How about ten o'clock?"

Erin said, "Fine. I'll see you then."

Jeff jogged over to town hall and went straight to Erin Clarke's office. She invited him to sit down. She opened the paperwork and pointed at the appraisal amounts. Jeff saw two lines. The top line said $118,000 and $145,000. The next line said $119,000 and $148,000. Underneath it said, "The average of the two appraisals as is: $118,500. The average of the two appraisals for remodeled value: $146,500." He assumed the town offered him the last number, $146,500.

A deep feeling of disgust hit Jeff in the pit of his stomach. That wasn't an offer; it was an insult. He was silent for a moment before he composed himself enough to put his anger into words.

"How do you expect me to give up my home for such a low amount when that doesn't even cover my mortgage?"

"Well, that's the average of the two appraisals."

He took the paperwork off her desk. "Let me look at these appraisals." He thumbed through them and saw the houses they'd compared his to. One sat on Park Avenue, a block away from the river. Another was on Princess Drive, three blocks away from the river. The third lay directly across the river, and Jeff knew it didn't have upgraded electric or plumbing, needed a new roof, and couldn't compare.

"I can't believe the house across the river sold for only $145,000," Jeff said. "If I would have known that, I would have bought it. These comparisons are insulting. How can you offer me such a little amount when those condos with the same square footage are selling for $480,000? An empty lot off Jefferson Boulevard on the river sells for $190,000, and a house up the river from me just sold for $440,000! This is ridiculous. My wife has said she won't take less than $350,000 for our house. My insurance company's replacement value is

$357,000. God forbid it would ever happen; there are too many treasures in my home I'd hate to lose, but I'd be further ahead if my house burned down and I'd still own the land! What am I supposed to do now?"

"Well, we have to wait for the engineers to get their plans drawn, and then we'll file a condemnation order against your home."

"When is that going to be?"

"Three to five years from now."

"You're kidding me. So, for the next three to five years, I have to keep investing money into a house you're going to tear down?"

"Well, I can't tell you what to do with your house," Erin said.

"How do you guys expect me to buy another house in my neighborhood for the amount you're offering me? You're kicking me out of my neighborhood!"

Erin pursed her lips and nodded her head. Jeff slammed his hand down on top of the paperwork, the room shook, then he picked it up. "God damn mother-fucking pieces of shit," Jeff said, loud enough everyone in town hall must have heard him. He stormed out.

One of Jeff's neighbors on the river, Jim Trent, had been the town's attorney in the past. Jeff went to his downtown office and asked to speak to Jim. Jim appeared in the background behind the receptionist.

"I don't know if you remember who I am," Jeff said, "but I'm Jeff Gray, one of your neighbors on the river. May I speak with you for a moment?'

"I'm waiting for a client," Jim told Jeff. "I've got some time." He took Jeff into a conference room with a long table and several large chairs. "Have a seat. What can I do for you?"

"Well, Jim, you're aware of what they're trying to do with the sidewalk going through your property," Jeff said. Jeff had seen him at the River Walk meeting. "I don't know if you knew this or not, but they plan on taking my house."

"You live at the end of Edgewater, right? In that white house next to the flower shop?"

"Yes; I've been restoring that house for seven years now." He told Jim, "They did two crappy appraisals on our house with only one river comp, and they're trying to steal our property from us. I don't know what to do next."

Jim replied, "Your property is worth whatever you say it's worth. It's just a matter of getting to court to prove it. You should take it to a jury trial."

"Really? How does that make things different?"

"Well, you know that property next to the Moonlight Inn on Franklin Pierce Road?"

"You mean where they put that park in?"

"Yeah, that's the place. Years ago, there was a case where the town took the owner of that property to court because they offered him $100,000 and the owner wanted $300,000. He told the jury it was worth three hundred thousand to him, and do you know what the jury came back with?"

"Three hundred thousand?" Jeff guessed.

"That's right," Jim said. "You get in front of a jury of your peers, and they won't want to let the town steal your property from you. I guarantee you the town officials won't let it get to that point, though. They'll make you a proper offer and settle before they let that happen."

Jim made a few phone calls and helped Jeff find an attorney who worked real estate law. Jim's client showed up, and Jeff thanked him and left the office.

When Kendra got home that night, Jeff told her about the offer. "I feel sick," she said. "If we take the offer, we won't even have our mortgage paid off, much less be able to buy another house."

"Well, I talked to Jim Trent, and he told me we have to get a jury trial."

"What does that do?" Kendra asked.

"He says a jury of our peers will be more likely to agree with us on the value of our property. He also said it won't get that far. The city will make us a proper offer before that happens. They can't do this to us; they're trying to screw us, and it isn't right. You know what this reminds me of?"

"What?" she asked.

"An experiment I read about when I took Psychology in college. They took a group of college students and told half of them to play the role of prison guards and the other half of them to play prisoners. They allowed the guards to lock up the prisoners and gave them uniforms, batons and everything."

"You mean Philip Zimbardo's Stanford prison study," Kendra chimed in.

"Yeah," he said. "Do you remember what happened?"

Kendra nodded. "The students who were assigned to play the guards became sadistic and lorded it over the prisoners. It was like they started thinking they really were prison guards, and they forgot it was an experiment."

"Exactly," Jeff said. "Someone told Jonathon Thompson, Justine Ernsberger, Erin Clarke and the rest of the mayor's staff they had a little bit of power so they're treating us, the citizens, like they're the prison guards and we're the prisoners. Not only have they lost sight of the fact that they're supposed to be public servants, they've also stopped practicing a free society form of government."

"What do you mean?" she asked.

"They're a bunch of Communists, or at least Socialists," he said. "They think what's theirs is theirs and what's mine is theirs too. They have no respect for our individual property rights anymore."

"We love the parks system; there's no doubt about that," Kendra said. "We don't love being kicked out of our neighborhood because of it. We were going to live here until we were ready to retire to Florida."

"I'm ready to get out of here," Jeff said. "I don't want to have a god damn thing to do with Princess City anymore. These people make me sick."

The next day he called one of the appraisers and told him about the low-ball offer the city had given him. "Why didn't you include any of the new construction when you wrote your comps?" Jeff asked.

"I'm not allowed to," the appraiser told him. "I have to compare your property to a like-aged property. Those condos are brand-new; your house is almost a century old."

"But you were inside my house, and you saw all the renovations we'd made. There's hardly a room left in my house still serving the same function it had when I moved in. I turned kitchens into bedrooms and bedrooms into kitchens. It may have been built in 1913, but my house is brand-new on the inside."

"I'm not allowed to take that into consideration," the appraiser told Jeff. "I wish I had better news for you, but the city will only accept my appraisals if I follow certain guidelines, and those guidelines have a lot to do with the comps I give them."

"But you only used one other property on the river," Jeff complained. "The only reason my property is so valuable to the city is because it's on the river. I know they're going to tear the house down, so it's mostly a question of the real estate the house is sitting on. Couldn't you have at least compared my house to some other houses where the people owned land on the water?"

"Mr. Gray," the appraiser said, "if I were you, I'd get a lawyer. I'd take the city to court to try and get what I thought my house was worth."

"I would, if I didn't think that would take at least three, if not four or five years," Jeff said. "I don't want to wait that long to know what my future is going to be. I need my fight with Princess City to end now."

He got off the phone, but the fact that he made payments on a property the town intended to tear down stuck at the front of Jeff's mind. Jeff and Kendra were stuck, unable to move on. He knew no one would buy the place once he disclosed Princess City intended to take it. The economy steadily got worse, and Jeff and Kendra had a harder and harder time keeping up with their bills.

Eighteen - Mockery
January, 2009

Kendra sat at the office chair in front of the computer, a stack of bills in front of her. "I know you're depressed about my brother and about the city taking the house, but we need to get some work soon," she told Jeff.

"I know," he said. "I just don't know how I'm going to do that when the phone hasn't been ringing."

"Thank God we got the credit union to defer our mortgage payments for this month and last month, because there's no way we would have been able to pay it," Kendra continued. "My paycheck every other week and the small jobs you get here and there are making it where we're just scraping by, but we're not getting any of our debts paid down. Next month, when we have to pay the mortgage again, I don't know how we're going to do it."

"I know one thing," Jeff said. "I will come up with something. The town's already laughing at us because we were expecting so much more from them than they're willing to pay for this house. Imagine what's going to happen if we can't make our mortgage payments and we lose the house. The credit union will have no problem selling the house to the city for whatever ridiculous low-ball offer they make; they'll be happy just to get something. Then the government will really have something to laugh about, and we'll be left filing bankruptcy on the rest of our mortgage."

"I could get a part-time job," Kendra said.

"It wouldn't be worth the gas money it would cost you to drive there. Not to mention all the extra time we'd be away from each other."

"I'm only trying to help."

"You keep doing what you're doing; at least the magazine is giving us some income. I'll go through all my customers in QuickBooks and call everyone to see if anyone has work for me. I'll also make some business cards and pass them out at all the real estate agents' offices. Even though home values are down at the moment, someone's loss is always someone else's gain, and these super-low home prices are keeping the real estate agents busy. If I could get a few remodeling jobs from them, it would help.

"The only thing is, most of my remodeling customers are older, retired people. They're the ones who are really not spending right now. They're the ones who've taken such a big loss in the stock market lately and the ones who'll be trying to hold on to as much of their money as they have left."

"It's worth a try," Kendra said. "We've got to try something; we can't sit around and wait for Erin Clarke to take our house."

While Kendra worked, Jeff did what he told her he would do. He sat in front of the computer with the phone and called every one of the customers he'd had any kind of long-term relationship with. He asked for any job he could get, no matter how small. They all told him the same thing: they had things they wanted done, but weren't willing to spend the money at the moment. Jeff printed off his business cards and delivered them to three different real estate offices he'd worked for in the past. He also left some at a flooring store and talked with the owner for a while. He let her know how badly he needed work. She told Jeff, "You look very professional. I'm used to a bunch of crackheads coming in, wanting work. Why don't you e-mail me your prices, and I'll see if I can find anything for you."

Jeff sat around the house all too often. He got a few small jobs, but they didn't pay enough to cover the bills. Between his struggles with Kendra's family and with the city, he could hardly motivate himself to get out to work.

On top of that, he felt his body beginning to break down. Some time between Lex's wedding and Isaac's, Jeff had begun having strange pains in his back. Some days, it hurt so much he didn't even want to get off the couch. He knew some of it was caused by stress, but more and more he began to wonder what was happening inside his body.

One day he couldn't stand the pain. Jeff had some pain killers left over from when he'd broken his foot a few years before. Even taking some of those didn't help. Jeff made an appointment to see his family doctor.

Dr. Anderson first asked, "How are you doing, Jeff? Are you still taking the anti-depressants?"

"I wasn't for a while," Jeff said. "Then my brother-in-law decided to make an ass of himself at his best friend's wedding and ostracized me from the family because of it. The city's taking my house, and the offer they made me was an insult. That, and the economy's going down the shitter, and nobody's hiring me to work on their houses anymore...I started taking them again a few weeks ago."

The doctor examined him. "Jeff, you're forty-one. You're getting older; it's not unusual for someone your age to have aches and pains, especially given the physically demanding work you do."

"This isn't just aches and pains," he told Dr. Anderson. "Something's wrong inside me; I can feel it."

Dr. Anderson located the tender spot on Jeff's lower back. "To be on the safe side, let's get you an ultrasound to see what's going on in there."

Jeff set up the appointment, and two weeks later Kendra took a day off to drive Jeff to his ultrasound appointment at the outpatient facility in Willow Bend.

"Did you see anything?" Jeff asked the tech when the test was over.

"Yeah," the tech said. "Your kidneys are covered in cysts. There are even some cysts growing on your liver. I didn't have to look very hard to find them; they were right there, impossible to miss, hundreds of them."

Jeff and Kendra's family doctor referred Jeff to a nephrologist, Dr. Singh, who said Jeff had polycystic kidney disease.

"I know my mom has a kidney disease," Jeff said. "She told me a long time ago I had a fifty-fifty chance of developing the same disease. I think she's on dialysis because of it. Is that what's going to happen to me?"

"Yes," Dr. Singh said. "Everyone who has this disease eventually has to either go on dialysis or get a kidney transplant. There is no cure for it, and it gets progressively worse until, eventually, your kidneys stop functioning. I could go in surgically and remove your cysts, or go in and drain the liquid from them--because that's what they are, little cysts filled with urine--but it wouldn't do you any good, because chances are they would grow right back."

"Are the cysts what cause the pain?" Jeff asked.

Dr. Singh shook his head. "The pain you've been experiencing intermittently is probably happening when one of the cysts presses against a rib."

"I'll give you one of my kidneys," Kendra volunteered.

Dr. Singh laughed. "That may be a possibility some time down the road, but that could be another fifteen, twenty years away. How old is your mother?"

"Sixty-two," Jeff said.

"If she's sixty-two now, and she just started having to be on dialysis, then you probably have at least twenty years before you have to worry about a transplant. In the meantime, though, I want you to do some tests so I can determine your present level of kidney functioning."

"What kinds of tests?"

Dr. Singh's assistant brought Jeff a large plastic jug. "This is a urine collection container," the doctor explained. "You use it every time you have to urinate for twenty-four hours, and then you bring the jug to the lab for analysis."

"What if I fill the jug before twenty-four hours are up?" Jeff asked. "I pee a lot."

"He does," Kendra said. "Sometimes he gets up two or three times a night."

"That doesn't happen very often," the doctor said. "You should be fine."

When the lab results came back, Dr. Singh determined Jeff's kidneys were failing. The doctor recommended he start dialysis treatments. Twice a week, Jeff went to dialysis. The pain bothered him daily, so Jeff looked into getting on disability. He found out he qualified, and decided to accept disability payments and retire from the remodeling business.

Shortly after his unofficial retirement, Jeff got the mail and found one of John Harrison's business cards in the mailbox. On the back was a hand-written note:

"Going to sell my house across the street. Interested in buying? Call me before I list. John"

Jeff wasn't interested in buying the house across the street, but he was interested to know what John planned to ask for it. He called the number on the card and asked, point-blank.

"Two hundred thousand," John said.

For the first time in months, Jeff felt hopeful. The house across the street was approximately the same square footage as Jeff and Kendra's, a little less if anything. It might have been a little nicer on the outside, the lawn a little more landscaped, but on the inside it was still an old house, without any of the improvements Jeff and Kendra made to theirs. If John managed to sell his house for two hundred, the city would have to value Jeff and Kendra's property at least that much…if not more, because of the newer interior. He told Kendra about it as soon as she came home from work.

"We're going to make the city a counter-offer, to see if they'll take it and get this shit over with," Jeff said. That night, he carefully composed the letter:

"Recently, the house across the street listed for $200,000. It needs some work done to it. The front facade is falling apart, and I'm sure it has some interior issues, also. I can't say how the owner justified $200,000, but that's what he came up with for his home.

"Currently, with our mortgage and personal debt (directly resulting from fixing our house), we owe $200,000, and would need $5000 for relocation. Our home is worth much more than that to us. We had future dreams and plans for our home that will never come to fruition. I used to say by the time I was old enough to retire, I was going to get half a million for it. We just want to move on with our lives. We've been depressed and sickened because of this whole matter.

"To allow the city to avoid attorney fees, court costs, and any additional relocation fees or punitive damages, we would like to offer our home to the city for $205,000."

Kendra proofread the letter for him and agreed it was acceptable. Jeff e-mailed one copy to Erin Clarke and another to Jonathon Thompson.

Jeff waited for a response, but after a week went by, he called Erin's office and asked to speak with her. "Did you receive our offer?" he asked her.

"Yes," Erin said.

"Well, do you accept it?"

"Mr. Gray," Erin said, "just because your neighbor's house is up for sale for $200,000 doesn't mean he's going to get $200,000 for it. I have a copy of your appraisal sitting on my desk right now, and the two appraisals averaged out to $118,500. That's the offer for your property."

"You're kidding me," he said. "All this time I thought your offer was $146,500."

"We never offered to pay you the remodeled value. Our offer was based on the property as-is. Your counter-offer is laughable, Jeff."

Jeff hung up, more certain than ever if he and Kendra waited for the city to buy the house, they were going to be screwed. Next he thought to bring media attention to his story, so he composed an editorial for the Willow Bend Tribune.

Jeff worked on his letter every morning and every evening for three days, having Kendra read it back to him over and over as he edited it and refined it into the best letter he'd ever written:

"Princess City is not practicing a free society government. The town of Princess City is currently telling us they are going to 'potentially' take our home as part of the River Walk in three to five years. It's going to happen, says

Erin Clarke (the town planner). At the Edgewater Drive meeting in the fall of '08, Mayor Jonathon Thompson stated he was going to take responsibility for taking the encroachment right to put a sidewalk through river property-owner's land, even over their combined objections. If you live on the river from Silver Park to Central Park (both sides), you're on notice: beware.

"We (my wife and I) thought we were going to be in our home into old age. They made us an offer 57% of the absolute minimum it would cost for us to pay off our house-related debt and be able to relocate. I'm a remodeler by trade and am constantly doing professional-grade improvements to our home. A two-car garage and deck to the river were planned. We even had plans for a pedal boat rental or kayak sales business. We know they're not going to pay us for our dreams, but we expect them to pay us for what we've put into it.

"We made a counter-offer which was less than half of what we expected we could get some day—a very fair deal— just to get things over with: our mortgage plus $5k. We don't want to pay taxes and interest on a house we're going to lose. We've given up working on finishing our 1913 home, because why should we work on something that's going to be torn down? We rarely landscape; we just don't care. It's caused a tremendous amount of stress on our marriage and many sleepless nights. We don't know when they'll take our house,

or where we'll live next. We know we're going to lose our home. . . that we pay for! We are constantly on red alert. They have already taken our home in our spirits and our minds. They have violated the sacredness of our home and hearth, and they are being allowed to continue this for the next three to five years, tentatively. It will never stop as long as we are in this home. It's a daily emotional struggle. We want to get away from this government. Enjoy your legacy, Jonathon Thompson.

"Sure, they're allowing us to use our court system years from now, but because of the Supreme Court ruling on eminent domain (July 2005, Kelo v. City of New London, CT), they've made us believe they will get away with taking our property. And by that time we will get what we asked for, plus at least 50% more, towards our true value of this property. As taxpayers, when do you want to buy our house? Now, or in the future, when it will cost you more? We don't understand the relocation committee's decision; it makes no sense from a business perspective. It's as though they want to make us suffer. They could've bought it when we did, when the ceilings were caved in and we had a waterfall in the kitchen every time it rained. Everyone else gave up on it. Jonathon Thompson said they were looking at it then. We bought it! It's my wife's Taj Mahal, a humble one but nonetheless. We rebuilt it.

"The city shouldn't have the right to do anything they think is going to benefit the community. Sure, our River Walk is beautiful, and is going to be grand once it goes through where our living room is and through untold numbers of homeowner's back yards. But where do we stop? We think the Union Street hill would make a great ski slope and would draw millions of dollars to our community. Should we threaten everyone there with the possibility of losing their homes to a ski slope because it would be good for the community? What if we put it right through Woodland Hills, where Erin Clarke's home is? It's scenic and off the beaten path. How about it, Erin Clarke? What if, in four years, we come and take your property for a ski slope? Think of the hotels and restaurants it would support, all of the employment that could be created. Your neighbors could have bed-and-breakfasts. Their property values would skyrocket. Or take your property and give it away for a dollar so a developer will build multi-million dollar homes and condos you can't afford. Growth for the sake of growth is the philosophy of cancer.

"Everyone should feel comfortable they are going to remain in their homes until their dying days. We should never be uneasy or unsure of where our home is in the United States of America. Everyone is at risk. Everyone.

"Our cities need to be able to plan and project, but there needs to be a willing consensus between the parties. If there is one holdout amongst a hundred, rather than destroying that person's environment, the other ninety-nine should have to provide that one can still maintain his island in the midst of their ocean. The one should never feel threatened and should always feel protected. That's equal freedom.

"It is so sad we have politicians and officials running our free government with Communistic rules. This is our land, and the bank's. We should not have city government that believes in these rules. It's un-American. Where is your patriotic conviction, Jonathon Thompson and Erin Clarke? Be Americans in spirit, not just in title.

"You damned Communists."

He signed it with his name and Kendra's, as he always did when he wrote anything that had to do with the house.

"You'll have to take off the 'damned Communists' part before you e-mail it to the newspaper," Kendra told him. Jeff hesitated, but agreed.

One day after sending his editorial, Jeff received a call from a Tribune reporter, Dave Burkholder. "This is definitely a newsworthy story," Dave assured him. "We'd like to consider this for an editorial, but we may want to do an article on you guys. Let me get a hold of my Princess City reporter, Angela Singer, and see what she wants to do with it."

"Great," Jeff said. "Should I call her?"

"I'll pass along your information, and she'll call you,"
Dave said. Once again, Jeff waited more than a week and still
got no reply. He called Angela and left two messages on her
answering machine before she got back with him.

"I'd like to interview you and your wife for a story in
the local section," Angela said.

"That's fine, as long as I can have final approval over
the story," Jeff said. "I want to make sure you're representing
my side of the story fairly."

"I can't give you final approval," Angela told him.
"Tribune policy." Jeff, wanting attention for what the city was
doing to them, reluctantly agreed.

One morning, Angela showed up and introduced
herself, then took a picture of Jeff and Kendra standing in front
of their home. After she took the picture, Jeff told Angela his
side of the story.

"I don't know if I want you to print this or not," Jeff
told her, "but I'm even thinking about running for mayor
against Jonathon Thompson. I don't know if I could win, or if
I'd even want to be mayor, but I'd damn sure try to make sure
the citizens of this town found about what he's really all about,
and I'd damn sure try to make it tough for him to get re-
elected."

Jeff woke at four the next morning; he couldn't get the
article out of his head. He hoped Angela would do a good job

with it, but somewhere in the back of his mind he suspected the article would not be in his favor. He got out of bed and went to the office to read the online version of the Tribune.

It was worse than he'd feared. Angela's article made Jeff and Kendra out to be a greedy couple who wanted an unreasonable amount of money for their run-down home. She mentioned Jeff wanting to run for mayor, but she didn't mention any of the qualifications he'd attached to his statement. She mentioned the city's offer of $118,500, but said nothing about the appraisal Jeff and Kendra had a few years before that placed the house's value at $188,000 before some of the most recent improvements, including the brand-new bathroom with a two-person shower on the first floor. Nor did she mention the house across the street, listed for $200,000, or the new condos on the same waterfront, with the same square footage, which began at $480,000. The article never said Jeff and Kendra couldn't buy a home in the same neighborhood for less than $250,000 to replace the one being taken away from them.

In fact, when she talked to Mayor Jonathon, Jonathon told Angela the town's interest in the property was only theoretical. "I'm not interested in purchasing that property," Angela quoted Jonathon as saying. "Maybe some mayor fifteen years from now will want it for the River Walk, but the Grays and I have been unable to reach an agreement."

"Liar," Jeff said out loud as he read the article. "Jonathon lied, and Angela made me look like an idiot. I never should have trusted her; I would've been better off having the Tribune print my editorial."

Kendra had managed to sleep through his conversation with himself, but Jeff couldn't help it. He went into the bedroom and woke her up. "Well, they butchered us," he said.

"Is the newspaper here already?" she asked, looking at the clock. "It's not even five in the morning yet."

"I read it online," Jeff said. "I'm sorry to bother you, but she made us look like idiots. She made it look like we were trying to screw the town instead of the other way around."

"What are we going to do next?" Kendra asked him.

"I don't know," Jeff said. "Now the mayor's saying he doesn't even want the house."

"That's good, right?" Kendra asked, sitting up.

"They're lying," Jeff said. "Jonathon says he doesn't want the house, yet Erin keeps assuring me this is inevitable. I know they're going to come after it again. And the next time they do, I'm going to slit their throats."

"Don't say that," Kendra said as she lay back down. "It scares me to imagine you could be that violent. I have to believe you're only venting, because I don't believe you would really do something like that."

"No, I wouldn't really do anything that violent." Jeff said. "I'm just furious; they've taken away my freedom."

Jeff didn't tell Kendra so, because he didn't want to worry her, but all kinds of revenge scenarios were floating through his mind.   He began making plans, plans he would never share with Kendra.

Nineteen - New Leaf
February, 2009

Jeff and Kendra sat on the couch one winter evening, watching TV. Kendra's mobile phone rang. "Who would be calling you this time of night?" Jeff asked.

"Probably another bill collector," she said. "Either that, or another relative who read about us in the newspaper." Angela's story had come out a month before, and Kendra's cousins were still calling about it. She picked up the phone. "Hello? Yes. Yes. Really?"

"Who is it?" Jeff whispered. Kendra raised her hand to shush him. She went into the office and returned a moment later.

"Who was that?" he asked again.

"Helena Boltmeyer, the editor of Midwestern Woman. She wants me to be their new assistant editor."

"Is that something you want to do?"

"Yeah!" Kendra said. "I've been trying for ages to get the Rock to promote me to editorial. I haven't had an outlet for my own writing since I worked for my college newspaper...this is exactly what I've been waiting for."

"Well, you're a great layout designer," Jeff said. "How much does this job pay? Hopefully it's more than what the magazine pays you."

"Helen is going to send me an e-mail with the job description and the salary," she said. "I'll check and see if I got it yet." She went to the computer, clicked the mouse a few times and said, "Wow, that's a real salary. It's going to be $60,000 a year."

"Holy shit!" he said. "That will more than make up for me having to go on disability." She'll be able to take care of herself without my help, Jeff thought.

"We'll be able to pay our mortgage and our other bills with that," Kendra said. "You won't even have to collect disability any more, and we'll finally be getting ahead."

"Not collect disability?" he said. "I've paid into it since I was fifteen years old. You'd better believe I'm going to collect it."

The thought of Kendra earning a decent wage relieved him. It meant they wouldn't have to worry about the credit union foreclosing on their house still several months away from the possibility, they nonetheless hadn't known how they would come up with the money.

Kendra called Helena the next morning and formally accepted the job. With Kendra's new salary, and the public declaration by the mayor that the town wasn't interested in the

Cedar Street house anymore, Jeff got inspired to work on his home again. He built the garage he and Kendra had dreamed of for the front of their house. Jeff did what he could, and subcontractors helped him with the rest. He had the front and back yards landscaped, with beautiful purple-leaved plum trees lining the path to the front door. On the north side and the back of the house, he built a wrap-around deck. It had a stairway down to the boat dock. They'd bought a fishing boat, and Jeff spent many of his days fishing for the king salmon that had eluded him for many years when he only fished from his pier.

By the middle of fall Jeff finished the deck. He and Kendra enjoyed the last warm nights of the year sitting by their outdoor fireplace, built into the deck. Looking out at the town lights over the river, they finally had a sense of peace.

Local elections came up in fall 2011. Mayor Jonathon Thompson ran against a Democratic candidate named Steve Wood. Normally Jeff hated voting by party. Jeff thought the party system was corrupt and hurting democracy. He would purposely vote for an independent just to strengthen a third party. Jeff and Kendra cast absentee ballots for Wood; they would be on a long-delayed vacation to Hawaii on the Tuesday in November when the election took place.

When Kendra started her new job, she'd started a vacation fund. She continued doing occasional layouts for the

River Rock, so the fund filled up quicker than she'd imagined. She worked from home now, so Jeff and Kendra were almost always together. One day, she turned from where she sat at her computer desk and said, "I just booked us a flight to Hawaii. I made hotel reservations and everything. It was cheaper than I'd expected, too, because it's the rainy season."

"Who cares about a little rain?" Jeff said. "We're going to Hawaii!"

Kendra explained she'd gotten them a hotel in Waikiki. She wanted to see Oahu because, as Jeff knew, her grandfather had been in the Navy and stationed at Pearl Harbor when the attack took place in 1941.

Kendra said, "I get to see the monument to the U. S. S. Arizona."

"That's the first thing we'll see when we get there," Jeff told her.

When they reached Oahu, Jeff and Kendra rented a car and drove from the airport in Honolulu to Waikiki, where they stayed on the ninth floor of the Halekulani Resort Hotel. From their balcony, they could see Diamond Head, the island's famous inactive volcano crater. They were fortunate enough to arrive on a sunny afternoon.

After a lunch of sashimi tuna at the resort's Orchids restaurant and a couple of beers, Jeff and Kendra went back to their room and took a nap. It was much later in Indiana than in

Hawaii, and the time difference took some getting used to. Then they took the forty-five minute trek to the U. S. S. Arizona Memorial.

They reached the memorial late that afternoon. Both stood in awe of it. The final resting place of hundreds of armed forces personnel, the Arizona memorial had a solemn air. Jeff and Kendra stood silent; Jeff couldn't seem to find words to express the emotions he felt. As a former sailor in the Navy, he could imagine vividly the horror the sailors experienced. Tears poured down his face. He looked at Kendra and saw her weeping also.

They listened to a tour guide narrate the statistics of what happened that fateful day. Jeff whispered to Kendra, "I don't know how much more of this I can take." He looked around and saw they weren't the only ones affected this deeply. Other men and women wept too.

On their second day in Hawaii, Jeff and Kendra hiked the trail around Diamond Head leading up the crater's rim. The hike lasted less than a mile, but the terrain consisted of a steep incline. When they reached the rim, they climbed the narrow, winding stairway to the deck of the observation tower. The view of the ocean and of Waikiki Beach amazed them. On their way back, though, Jeff and Kendra's good luck with the weather came to an end, and it started to rain.

In the evening, they had dinner at another of the resort's restaurants, then went into downtown Honolulu, where they toured the bars. They left the rental car in an overnight garage, drank all the beer and fruity umbrella drinks they wanted, and took a cab back to their resort.

The next day, Jeff and Kendra checked out of the Halekulani. They took a small plane to the Big Island, where they witnessed a lava flow at Volcanoes National Park. That night they walked, naked, on the black sand beach at Punaluu. They saw the endangered turtles and even saw dolphins in the waters off the beach.

"Do we have to go back?" Kendra asked Jeff as they took shelter underneath a beach umbrella. It had started to rain again, though lightly compared to the downpour at Diamond Head.

"Yes," he said. "We have bills to pay, and a house to take care of. Besides, I'm sure your mom and dad don't want to baby-sit the cat forever."

"I do miss Applesauce," Kendra said. "But for a little while, let's pretend we live here."

"Well, you can always ask Helena if she'd be willing to put up with you being on a five or six hour time difference from her. You could do your editing from here."

"We could rent a house," Kendra said. "What was that you said when we were thinking about moving here? That there are ramshackle houses on the Big Island we could afford?"

"Some of the rents are pretty cheap here. We could afford them if we sold our house," Jeff said.

"Well, it's really nice now. I'm sure we could find a buyer, but what about the city?"

"The city said they're not interested in it, so we don't have a disclosure problem now. We could sell it to anyone."

Jeff explained to Kendra all the things he'd researched about buying an unpermitted house, shacks that aren't to code so they can't be financed by a bank, but could be purchased on land contracts. They could either buy an unpermitted house, or they could rent, he told her.

Over the next two weeks, they snorkeled, explored volcanoes and rain forests, ate incredible Japanese food and hung around on the beaches. Jeff kept wanting to go back to the black sand beach where they could walk around naked. Kendra had one rule during their heavenly vacation: Jeff was forbidden to think about Princess City. Jeff tried hard to forget what the mayor and the city planner tried to do to them.

Leaving Hawaii was like walking out through the gates of heaven. They both knew returning to Princess City would be a disappointment. "Well, at least we get to see Applesauce," Kendra said groggily as they took off from LAX.

They arrived home and unpacked. Candace had stacked the mail on the coffee table. Kendra flipped through it and found another letter from the city. She opened it. "What does it say?" Jeff asked her.

"It's a letter of condemnation," she told him. "They're taking our house. They want us out."

Mayor Jonathon Thompson, it seemed, had won his bid for re-election. According to the Tribune, it wasn't even a close race. Jeff wondered if anyone remembered Angela Singer's article, and how the mayor said he didn't want the Grays' house anymore, or if anyone cared he had blatantly lied. He couldn't complain to the Tribune; they were on the mayor's side. In fact, since the interview, Jeff had learned Angela got her press releases and information about the city from the mayor's secretary, Rachelle, who made her up a packet of information weekly. No wonder Angela wasn't willing to rock the boat with Mayor Thompson.

There were no other newspapers in the town, nor in the next city over. The Tribune serviced both, and was owned by the same out-of-town media corporation that owned the River Rock. There was no one left to complain to.

The next day, while Kendra worked on the magazine from home, Jeff did something he had never done before in his life: he went to the gun shop. He didn't tell Kendra where he was going.

"May I help you?" the man behind the counter asked as Jeff looked around him, bewildered by the variety of firearms.

"Yeah. I want to buy a shotgun."

The man behind the counter eyed Jeff. "What are you going to use it for?"

"Goose hunting, rabbit hunting, maybe some squirrel. I remember a friend of mine having one with an interchangeable barrel. I think it was called a Deerslayer."

"That's a nice gun. We've got three of those in stock."

"I'd like to see one," Jeff said.

"Right this way," the dealer said. He directed Jeff to the rack of shotguns. He took out a key and unlocked a cable that went through all the triggers. He pulled down a 20-gauge Remington Deerslayer. He checked the chamber and showed Jeff it was unloaded, showed him how some of the other parts functioned, and handed it over to Jeff.

The stock was made out of a dark-stained wood with a rubber sole at the end of it. The barrel and firing mechanism were blue steel that reflected like a dark mirror. Jeff held it up to his shoulder and pointed it up at a deer head mounted on the wall.

"Is it okay to dry-fire it, or will that hurt it? I've heard before you can hurt a gun doing that."

"It's not something you want to make a habit of," the dealer said. "But go ahead. You'll be fine."

Jeff put his left hand on the piece of wood that cradled the barrel, pulled it toward him, then released it. Chook-chook: he cocked the gun. Keeping his left hand in that position, Jeff pointed the gun up at a goose decoy in the corner of the room. Click; he pulled the trigger.

"This one'll be fine," Jeff said. "This is a nice gun."

"We'll have to fill out some paperwork," the dealer said. "I'll need to see your ID. In a couple days you can come pick it up."

A few days later, Kendra told Jeff, "I have to attend a web developers' conference for the magazine. It's in Joliet, Illinois. Should I go ahead and book us a hotel room now?"

"Get a hotel room for yourself," Jeff said. "I won't be going with you."

"Why not?" Kendra asked. "You always go with me. The entire time we've been married, you and I have never spent a night apart. What, do you have something better to do?"

"Not something better," he said. "I have an appointment with the nephrologist that Friday. You know how hard it is to get an appointment with him, and I have been feeling pretty sore lately."

"Oh," she said, sounding disappointed. "Are you sure you don't want me to tell Helena I can't make the conference so I can go to your doctor visit with you?"

"No," he said. "If your boss wants you to go, then go. I'm sure you'll meet a lot of good contacts, and you'll have a good time. I trust you."

"I trust you, too," she said.

"I wish I could go, but this is just one of those sacrifices we're going to have to make. We both knew we'd have to spend a night apart from each other eventually."

"Yeah," she said, "but I was hoping it wouldn't happen for a long, long time."

"I was, too," Jeff said. "But then I got sick." She stood up from her computer chair, put her arms around him, and nuzzled his shoulder. They embraced for a long while before Jeff let go of her.

Twenty - Death's Day
December 2011

At the top of the stairs, Earl pulled the fire alarm. He made it to the second floor of town hall before he roared at the top of his lungs, with spit flying, "Get out of the building!" People ran in every direction, panicking, screaming in their frantic efforts to get out of a situation they didn't understand.

The fire alarm blared, and the fire department arrived moments later. All the local fire departments responded to the building fire. Earl heard sirens from all over the city, not only fire trucks but also squad cars. The police showed up to do traffic control for the fire department; they hadn't gotten the message about the possible hostage situation yet. Earl watched out the window as fire fighters entered the building with the hose.

Earl raced out of the building. To the first police officer he saw, directing traffic away from town hall on the road directly in front of the side door, Earl said, "Hey, this is a hostage situation! What are you guys doing?"

"What are you talking about?" the officer asked him.

"That crazy fucker Jeff Gray drove his car through the doors and set it on fire! Didn't you see the busted-out doors on the east side? I tried to shoot him, but I missed."

The officer took Earl to his sergeant, who had Earl repeat his story. The sergeant picked up his radio, called the dispatcher, and said, "We've got a possible hostage situation; tell all units to cancel signal ten!"

As a former member of the police force, Earl knew "cancel signal ten" meant no lights and sirens. As if Jeff didn't already know the police were coming for him. It was too little, too late.

*****

The sergeant went into the building and yelled at all the fire fighters. "Get the hell out of here!" he screamed at them. "This is a hostage situation."

The hose captain told his men, "Hold your line! We've almost got it!"

"I said get out of here, god damn it!" the sergeant yelled.

"Get out of our way!" the hose captain said. "We've almost got it, and we're not going to lose this building." The hall filled with thick, black smoke. "Now you need to get out of here; you don't even have a respirator on!"

The sergeant retreated, coughing.

Once the hose team had succeeded in dowsing the burning car, the hose captain yelled, "Now let's get out of here!" They evacuated the building. The car steamed, but the fire had been put out.

Outside town hall, the police hurried to get all the civilians and the fire fighters out of the area. The fire fighters left their trucks in place as a barrier. The police directed traffic and called the county to send the SWAT Team. In forty-five minutes the SWAT Team arrived.

When the SWAT Team arrived, they isolated the telephone lines so Jeff could no longer dial out and set up their command center. Captain Michael Fisher, the Officer in Charge, called in and phoned Jeff.

"What does he want?" one of Fisher's subordinates asked when the call ended.

"He wants to talk to the media, but I'm not going to let him. Somebody get me eyes in there! I need to see what's going on in that office. Conrad, you get on that roof and find a way to get a camera in through the ceiling of that office. Laurence and Cooper, you two set up sniper posts there and there." He pointed to some houses across the street. "Beck, attach a microphone to the window of that office so we can hear what's going on."

Conrad got onto the roof. From there, he snaked a camera through one of the vents into the mayor's office.

Once the SWAT Team had eyes, Conrad called Fisher and showed him the monitor. They realized the mayor lay unconscious. He may already have been dead; Fisher couldn't tell. "God damn it!" Fisher shouted. "Let's get in there. Now!"

A team of five tactical officers gathered at the door, "nut's to butt's" they called it, with the battering ram.

Fisher could see on the camera that Jeff was practicing suicide, putting the barrel of the gun into his mouth from different angles. Whether he had the balls to do it or not, Fisher didn't know, but he couldn't take that chance.

"Come on, hurry up!" he radioed to the tactical team. "Get it together. We've got to get in there now!"

*****

As he stood over the mayor, Jeff decided his time was almost up, and he'd better at least make sure Jonathon was dead. Jeff thought he'd always heard in the Mafia movies, "One in the head and one in the heart."

He pulled the trigger of the handgun; he would shoot the mayor in the head first. The window broke, and a flash bang went off. The bullet lacerated the side of his head while Jeff fell to the ground.

Jeff, knocked on his ass, got disoriented. Pissed off, he staggered back to his feet. How dare they come for him now, when he'd almost completed the job? The only thing left to do was kill Jonathon. Jeff didn't care what happened to him anymore. All he cared about was that Jonathon would rot in hell.

The battering ram burst through the barricaded door as Jeff staggered over to the mayor, aiming to shoot Jonathon in the head. The bullet wouldn't glance off this time.

One member of the tactical team fired off three shots. Jeff felt a searing pain the moment before the world went black.

*****

"Shooter is down," the tactical team reported to Fisher. "Confirmed kill. The shooter is down."

"Is Thompson alive?" Fisher asked.

"I can't tell," the tactical officer responded.

"Somebody get a medic," Fisher said, "and the coroner." Fisher sent the EMTs into the building.

*****

At the official dedication ceremony three years later, a delegation of city council members and the relocation committee, including Erin Clarke, walked the entire length of the north bank of the River Walk, from Logan Street to Princess Avenue. At Cedar Street, they paused where Jeff and Kendra's house had once stood.

Before a pristine, new sidewalk, with a red ribbon in hand, the president of the county council stood beside the president of the city council, the presidents of the development and construction companies and Mayor Jonathon. Jonathon Thompson had stayed in the intensive care unit for a week, and then spent another month in the hospital. He had survived.

"It's amazing to think there used to be a living room here," the city council president said.

Jonathon winced, remembering the fear.

*****

Kendra read the Tribune's online news story about the River Walk's opening on her laptop, then logged off and closed it. She drummed her fingers on the wooden tabletop for a moment before a young waitress in a hula skirt came over and asked her if she wanted something to drink.

"I'll have a Mai tai," Kendra said. The appeal of tropical drinks hadn't quite worn off on her yet, though she knew she'd have to rein in her spending soon. She'd just started her new job with Pacific Appeal magazine, and after she'd settled with Princess City over Jeff's estate, she had to start again from virtually nothing.

As the waitress walked away, Kendra looked out across the beach. A smattering of gray clouds kept the sun from overpowering her eyes as she looked out at the glassy ocean.

Small waves lapped the beach as disappointed surfers tossed a soft football around and kicked the sand.

The man from the table next to Kendra's leaned back in his chair. He was about Kendra's age, a tall man with long limbs, gingerbread-colored skin, and glossy black hair. "I haven't seen you before," he said."Did you come from the mainland?"

"Yeah. Indiana."

"So what brought you here?"

The waitress set a drink in front of Kendra and asked if she wanted anything else. Kendra took a sip and shook her head.

"It's a long story," she said.

"I've got time." the man said. "With a woman as pretty as you telling it, it must be interesting."

The End

Kelo v. New London

Lawsuit Challenging Eminent Domain Abuse in New London,
Connecticut

By The Institute for Justice. Reprinted with permission.

Susette Kelo dreamed of owning a home that looked out over the water. She purchased and lovingly restored her little pink house where the Thames River meets the Long Island Sound in 1997, and had enjoyed the great view from its windows.

Tragically, the City of New London turned that dream into a nightmare.

In 1998, pharmaceutical giant Pfizer built a plant next to Fort Trumbull and the City determined that someone else could make better use of the land than the Fort Trumbull residents. The City handed over its power of eminent domain—the ability to take private property for public use—to the New London Development Corporation (NLDC), a private body, to take the entire neighborhood for private development. As the Fort Trumbull neighbors found out, when private entities wield government's awesome power of eminent domain and can justify taking property with the nebulous claim of "economic development," all homeowners are in trouble.

The fight over Fort Trumbull eventually reached the U. S. Supreme Court, where the Court in 2005, in one of the most controversial rulings in its history, held that economic development was a "public use" under the Fifth Amendment to the U. S. Constitution.

The Supreme Court's 5-4 decision against Kelo and her neighbors sparked a nation-wide backlash against eminent domain abuse, leading eight state supreme courts and 43 state legislatures to strengthen protections for property rights. Moreover, Kelo educated the public about eminent domain abuse, and polls consistently show that Americans are overwhelmingly opposed to Kelo and support efforts to change the law to better protect home and small business owners. Moreover, in the five years since the Kelo decision, citizen activists have defeated 44 projects that sought to abuse eminent domain for private development.

Meanwhile, in New London, the Fort Trumbull project has been a dismal failure. After spending close to 80 million in taxpayer money, there has been no new construction whatsoever and the neighborhood is now a barren field. In 2009, Pfizer, the lynchpin of the disastrous economic development plan, announced that it was leaving New London for good, just as its tax breaks are set to expire.

But Susette Kelo's iconic little pink house was saved and moved to a new location. You can visit the historic, Kelo

House, which is now the home of local preservationist Avner Gregory, at its new location in downtown New London: 36 Franklin Street (at the intersection of Franklin and Cottage Streets).

For a compelling account of the history and back-story of the New London controversy, read Jeff Benedict's "Little Pink House: A True Story of Defiance and Courage" published in 2009 by Grand Central Publishing.

"The specter of condemnation hangs over all property. Nothing is to prevent the State from replacing any Motel 6 with a Ritz-Carlton, any home with a shopping mall, or any farm with   a   factory.
—Justice Sandra Day O'Connor

The Fifth Amendment to the Constitution of the United States of America is known as the Trial and Punishment and Compensation for Takings amendment. It states, in part, "No person shall…. be deprived of life, liberty, or property, without due process of law; nor shall private property be taken for public use, without just compensation." This amendment was ratified in 1791.

Real estate developer and author Don Corace writes in his book Government Pirates: The Assault on Private Property Rights and How We Can Fight It, "Even many of the citizens who have had their property unfairly seized and handed over to private developers can agree with the long-held standard that eminent domain can, and should, be used for building roads, dams, airports, schools, military bases, and other necessary public uses as long as owners are fairly compensated."

"Necessary public uses" and "fairly compensated" are the key words. In 2005, the U. S. Supreme Court ruled in the case of Kelo v. New London, Connecticut that promoting economic development is a fair use of eminent domain. The decision was split, four justices to five. Commentators, including Corace, have suggested that the ruling gives too much power to municipalities (and private developers) and oversteps the bounds of individual citizens' property rights.

Note that in the Kelo case, the city of New London acted through the New London Development Corporation, a privately owned, non-profit organization. Many see the delegation of the governmental power of seizure to third-party corporations as eminent domain abuse in and of itself. In other parts of the country, waterfront homes worth $1 million or more have been designated "blighted" in order to justify eminent domain. Wherever greed and corruption are possible, so is eminent domain abuse.

The authors of this fictional work do not advocate violence. Romans 12 (NIV):

"(14) Bless those who persecute you; bless and do not curse. (15) Rejoice with those who rejoice; mourn with those who mourn. (16) Live in harmony with one another. Do not be proud, but be willing to associate with people of low position. Do not be conceited.

"(17) Do not repay anyone evil for evil. Be careful to do what is right in the eyes of everybody. (18) If it is possible, as far as it depends on you, live at peace with everyone. Do not take revenge, my friends, but leave room for God's wrath, for it is written, 'It is mine to avenge; I will repay,' (Deut 32:35) says the Lord. (20) On the contrary: 'If your enemy is hungry, feed him; if he is thirsty, give him something to drink. In doing this, you will heap burning coals on his head' (Proverbs 25:21-22).

"(21) Do not be overcome by evil, but overcome evil with good."

ABOUT THE AUTHORS

TIT ELINGTIN

Tit Elingtin is a warrior by nature. He loves deep and hard. Tit expects his friends to be loyal to the truth above all. He describes his philosophical views like this: "As the river flows, it is as one. We are as the mist of the waterfall, joining others and separating as we fall to be one with the river once again."

ERIN O'RIORDAN

Erin O'Riordan lives in the Midwestern United States with her husband and co-author Tit Elingtin. Her short stories, essays, and film reviews have been published in numerous magazines and websites. Readers can view more of her work at www. aeess. com.

If you enjoyed EMINENT DOMAIN,

you might also enjoy:

THE SMELL OF GAS

By Erin O'Riordan and Tit Elingtin

April 2011 from Melange Books

http://www. melange-books. com/

Love pulp fiction? Just try putting down The Smell of Gas. TSOG is full of saints and sinners you'll love to hate. There's Brigid, the high school basketball player and secret heroin addict. Fred, a Catholic lesbian teen, loves Brigid, but doesn't know about her affair with Edward, a married Evangelical preacher. Sex, ethics, religions and mythologies clash as you dig deeper into their connection to the death of a young couple. Excerpt from The Smell of Gas:

January 2000

In Fred's bright white room, she'd stacked three rows of votive candles in red jars on her dresser. Fred's roommate, Leander, said they reminded him of the cemetery, but Fred used them as a meditation point when she prayed.

She liked the deep blue sheets on her bed. The white-and-blue color scheme matched the dress and cape of the woman in the poster above Fred's bed. The print of Murillo's Immaculate Conception of the Escorial, painted in 1678, portrayed the Virgin, eyes looking up to heaven, surrounded by cherubim and standing on a crescent moon. Behind the Virgin's head, the cherubim dissolved into an orange haze. In the light of the burning votives, the whole room seemed to glow orange.

Three rows of seven candles before her, she said one Hail Mary for each.

Fred finished saying her twenty-first Hail Mary and got off her knees. She blew out all of the candles except one. The cheap candles smoked, filling Fred's small bedroom with a grayness that reminded her of an underwater scene. She walked over to the bed and lifted the corner of the mattress. She had to grope for a moment to find it, tucked inside the elastic of the blue fitted sheet's corner. She held up the razor to the candlelight. The blood left on it from the last time didn't bother her. It was clean blood, her own.

If you enjoyed EMINENT DOMAIN
you might also enjoy:

BELTANE

Pagan Spirits, Book One

Eternal Press, 2009

By Erin O'Riordan

Twin sisters Allie and Zen have always shared everything: including an unconventional upbringing at Pagan Spirits Farms. They even fall in love at the same time. Pagan priestess Allie thinks she's met the man of her dreams in her buttoned-down lawyer fiancé, Paul Phillip. But is he everything he seems? Zen, a witch gifted with the sixth sense, falls for Orlando. But there's a catch: Orlando is married to someone else. As the celebration of Beltane nears, the sisters seem destined to be unlucky in love. But the Goddess moves in mysterious ways, and May Day may turn out to be magic for them after all.

MIDSUMMER NIGHT

Pagan Spirits, Book Two

April 2011

By Erin O'Riordan

Priestess-in-training and part-time witch Zen Van Zandt loves biology grad student Ramesh Sudhra. Only two things stand in the way of their happiness: his traditional Indian-American family doesn't welcome Zen, and Zen's training requires a yearlong vow of celibacy. Between Ramesh's mother's disapproval, Zen's vow of celibacy and her assistant's romantic troubles with a wild new witch, Zen wonders if she and Ramesh will ever see their wedding day.

SAINT JAMES' DAY

Pagan Spirits, Book Two

Coming Soon

By Erin O'Riordan

While her boss is away on her honeymoon, young witch Gillian wonders if she'll ever get her chance to fall in love. The love of her life left with her money, and her best friend Mike has fallen in love with Trina, a waitress at their favorite hang-out. Gillian's attracted to newcomer James, but they seem like an unlikely couple, since he's a born-again Christian and may not share her open-minded point of view. Will she pine away for what could have been with her lost love, take a chance on James, or make a bold play to start a whole new relationship with Mike? It'll take a crystal ball to predict this contemporary, magical romance.

61058249R00156

Made in the USA
Middletown, DE
18 August 2019